Tag goes here

Cover copy goes here

Books by Aubrie Dionne

Nebula's Music
Messenger In the Mist
Minstrel's Serenade

Published by Kensington Publishing Corporation

Messenger In the Mist

Aubrie Dionne

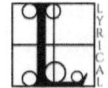

LYRICAL PRESS
Kensington Publishing Corp.
www.kensingtonbooks.com

Lyrical Press books are published by
Kensington Publishing Corp. 119 West 40th Street New York, NY 10018

All Kensington titles, imprints, and distributed lines are available at special
quantity discounts for bulk purchases for sales promotion, premiums, fund-
raising, and educational or institutional use.

Special book excerpts or customized printings can also be created to fit
specific needs. For details, write or phone the office of the Kensington
Special Sales Manager:
Kensington Publishing Corp.
119 West 40th Street
New York, NY 10018
Attn. Special Sales Department. Phone: 1-800-221-2647.

First Electronic Edition: Jully 2010
eISBN-13: 978-1-61650-171-6
eISBN-10: 1-61650-171-5

First Print Edition: July 2010
ISBN-13: 978-1-61650-865-4
ISBN-10: 1-61650-865-5

Printed in the United States of America

To my mom, Joanne, for always believing in me.

Acknowledgements

First of all, I want to thank Lyrical Press for believing in my writing! Next, my wonderful editor, Stef Szymanski, who always pushed me to make my story shine. My critique partners, Christine Rains and Cherie Reich, have provided a wealth of support along with my top beta readers: my sister, Brianne and my mom, Joanne. Lastly, a big thanks goes out to my husband, Chris, for putting up with all my crazy story ideas at the dinner table!

Chapter 1
Lost Soul

Star secured her pack bag to Windracer's saddle, trying not to think about the giant beasts waiting outside the grid. Evenspark's mist blowers towered over her like giant toadstools, chugging and sputtering wind above the city line. Every journey began with this cacophony, stirring acidic anxiety in her stomach.

She struggled to quell her raging nerves, running a shaky hand through her horse's mane. She reminded herself of her obligations, her goals and her dreams. Everything she ever wanted lay beyond the metal gate. All she had to do was ride.

The shriek of her superior's voice shot through the clamoring to rouse Star from her haunted reverie. "On with you, now! No more pestering the collectors. If people's letters didn't reach us, they'll just have to hold their tongues until the next messenger gets back."

"Yes, Zetta." Star inspected Windracer's hooves, each one the span of two of her hands put together. She straightened, meeting Zetta's cheeky gaze with her own steadfast gray eyes. "I'm ready."

"Come then. You should ride out before the darkness sets in."

Zetta shuffled her through the first checkpoint, barely allowing Star time to sign the departure papers for each of the duty guards. Star shoved several bundled messages, rolled scrolls and hasty scribblings into her leather bag, stuffing it full until the front flap barely fastened.

Her superior followed like a fly, instructing her every breath of the way. "Never venture off course, not for anything or anyone. Your job is to deliver the correspondence and nothing more."

"Yes, Zetta," Star answered for the 122nd time before her 122nd run. She tried not to be annoyed by customary procedures, even if they took extra time.

"And don't get caught up in unexpected meetings or activities. We need you back here in two days."

Star tore herself away from signing the last of her departure papers to bow, her moonlight hair falling around her shoulders. "Understood."

High-strung as a laundry line, Zetta tapped on Star's letter bag. Usually her tirade stopped before the ring of mist blowers. However, this time she followed Star to the edge of the grid.

Without the currents of air to keep the mist at bay, the wispy tendrils of fog unfurled between them, obscuring Zetta's sharp-nosed features in a ghost-like air. Star turned to Windracer, but Zetta's voice held her still.

"There is one more item to dispatch." From deep within the folds of her tunic, Zetta pulled out a small letter with an unidentifiable seal. "This goes too."

An alarm bell rang in Star's head and she paused. Zetta defied protocol. All letters had to be processed, tracked and signed by the head collector. "But this hasn't—"

"I know." Zetta averted her eyes. Star wondered if her superior pretended to be preoccupied with the lands lurking beyond the metalwork of the grid as an excuse to avoid her gaze. "There is not enough time for this letter's review. I have orders by a higher power to allow it through immediately. My job and yours are on the line."

Star fought a questioning retort. She took the folded paper in her hand, smoothing her thumb over the seal. The stock looked thick and expensive, stamped with the symbol of a man slaying a great flying beast. The stenciled letters on the front read *Fallon Leer* and the address of a lowly residence in the outskirts of Ravencliff. Star did not recognize the name, but treachery and desperation plagued the destination's streets.

She mounted Windracer in one swift motion, her body light and agile as a swan taking flight. Windracer's back towered over Zetta's head and Star had to look down to address her superior. "I'll make sure the letter is received."

Zetta signaled to the guards and the doors of the grid unlatched, the intertwining strands of metal screeching as they pulled apart to reveal a countryside drowned in mist. The smoky wisps choked the moors surrounding Evenspark in an ominous miasma, flowing steadily across the ground like a disease. Star imagined it as an eternal shroud clinging to the land, a looming veil engulfing the heedless wanderer in a world of nothingness where twilight reined supreme.

Zetta's gaze changed from watchful to pensive. "The queen's guards reported another disappearance this morning—a man repairing the grid."

Star tightened the reigns around her wrists. "The Elyndra won't catch me. I'm too fast."

Her superior nodded. "Just as well, be careful."

"You know I always am." With a shout, Star dug her heels in Windracer's sides. The horse's flanks heaved in a whirlwind of motion, springing to a full-fledged gallop. Her massive hooves dug deep impressions in the muddied ground.

The mist swirled in around them as they followed the narrow trail winding into the abyss of deep vales surrounding Evenspark. As she rode, Star clutched her leather bag close to her chest as if her heart beat inside it.

As if her imagination summoned one of them, a distant rustling swirled the wind above her head. Star ducked in her saddle, burying her face in Windracer's mane. Although she'd never seen one, travelers described the Elyndra as iridescent behemoths spanning the width of two wagons put together. Now she rode through their domain.

Refusing to be frightened by the beasts hovering in wait, Star turned to more alluring thoughts. Every hoofbeat carried her closer to Ravencliff and Prince Valen. The memory of his sharp-edged face and keen eyes brought a rush of warmth to her cheeks, belying the cold.

During her last visit, she caught him watching her in the crowded hallways of the inner sanctuary. His eyebrows had curved in a wistful look, as if he'd known her from long ago. She, too, had experienced a flare of recognition. Although the question of why a prince would ever meet a lowly messenger girl remained to be solved.

She would get a chance to speak to him if she possessed a certain kind of letter. Messengers were only allowed in royal quarters if they held matters of business. Star felt the weight of the leather bag against her chest. Because of Zetta's fretting, she'd not have the time to identify the recipients. She knew the possibilities of possessing such a letter were slim, but she could always hope. Optimism carried her during these journeys, along with hopes and dreams that someday she would earn enough gold to keep her parents safe, and someday she would steal a decent conversation with the prince.

Star languished in distant daydreams throughout the course of her journey until she rode the last stretch before Ravencliff's walls. A plaintive wail rang throughout the landscape like the last utterance of a tortured soul. Her thoughts snapped back to the present, returning from rosy diversions to diaphanous mist and waning light. The squeal had been high-pitched and faint, as if something small called out in alarm and played on her heart like melancholy tones plucked from a delicate lyre. How could she ignore it?

Impossible. Nothing could survive outside of the fortress walls, at least not for long, unless it had recently run off. Star balked at the thought of any means of escape from Ravencliff. Carved from the black onyx of Mount Clawmark, the sheer edifice rose hundreds of feet from the earth, impenetrable from inside or out. Anything or anyone who wished to leave would face a regiment of guards and a drawbridge as broad as an ancient Blackwood.

The sound, a definite and desperate call for help, wafted from ahead. The rhythmic beat of Windracer's hooves echoed in Star's ears as they trod the damp earth. Usually the hoofbeats were enough to fill the silence. However, now she listened for more.

Never venture off course, Zetta's voice screamed in her memory. *Not for anything or anyone.*

Despite the dire warning, Star's interest grew with each galloping step. She chanced a look up at the sky. Nothing but mist hung above her head, and beyond that, endless clouds of gray. Star hadn't felt the fluttering of the wings for some time now, and assumed the previous scare was probably a result of her wandering imagination.

Cursing her curiosity, Star pulled back on the reins. Windracer's pace slowed to a canter, the horse's deep heaves of breath pluming in the air from lungs as big as two pillows. The mist pressed in on them as an omnipresent force. Star listened for the giant undulations stirred by the Elyndras' wings, the sound deep and airy like the spreading of a quilt, but silence prevailed. She had a few tenuous moments at best.

A raised path of beaten-down soil substituted for a road. Tall grasses and cattails surrounded the mound of dirt, as if the marsh reached out to reclaim the scar of land. She could not venture far. Her boots rose past her knees, but there was no telling how far down the bog sank.

Star did not know what would kill her first: drowning in the sludge or the hovering beasts that could pluck her from the bog with their slew of spindly legs. Suppressing a shudder, she dismounted and edged to the side of the road.

Windracer's eyes rolled. She could sense danger from long distances. Star patted her on the nose. "It's okay, girl, I'm not going far."

Star stepped cautiously along the edge of the road, scanning the tall cattails for any sign of life. Up ahead, the grass shook. Something moved beneath the long stalks. Star took a deep breath, convincing herself the animal was too small to be anything threatening. She crept closer, her boots sticking in the muck. The air reeked of sour rot and dank wood. She covered her mouth with her sleeve.

When Star reached an arm's length from the thicket, she crouched close to the ground, teetering, and swept back the long stems of swamp weed. An animal she least expected to see huddled underneath a mossy protrusion of rock. "A bunnyfly?"

Was this an elaborate hoax? Star took a step back, disbelieving. What was a bunnyfly doing out in the middle of nowhere, in hostile territory, no less? Originally scavengers, the fluttery animals were bred for centuries as play objects for rich children. They had no innate defenses or known purpose on the planet besides being adorable.

The animal flitted its glittery wings when it saw her and retreated further back in the crevice between the rock and the muddied earth. If she moved too quickly, she would scare the animal away and never get hold of it. Although the wings were more for show than anything else, it could hop large distances in a short amount of time.

Though the lost pet could scurry around fast, it would only survive the Elyndra for so long. Star felt compelled to save the bunnyfly. She checked on Windracer with a glance over her shoulder. The horse's outline cast a slight black shadow in the mist, making both of them sitting targets. If the Elyndra took her horse, she would have no chance at survival. She could not tarry.

Bending down closer to the rock, Star cooed and sang to the bunnyfly, reaching out slowly with her hand. If only she knew its name. They usually responded when called. The animal edged back farther in the crevice, its floppy ears covering the front paws like velvet curtains.

Star remembered the piece of pastry bread stowed away in her cloak for a snack. Long journeys like this always made her hungry. Thankfully, she had packed provisions. With one hand, Star reached in her front pocket, crumbling the bread into small pieces. The bunnyfly sniffed the sugary scent right away, its large, innocent eyes changing from fearful to intrigued. Its nose crinkled, whiskers twitching.

"Come on, darling." Star coaxed it out of the hole with a trail of sweet crumbs, leading to her coat pocket.

As soon as the bunnyfly chanced a hop closer, Star grabbed it with both hands, trying to be gentle but firm so it wouldn't slip from her long fingers as she slid it between her coat and her blouse. She would have glitter and fur all over her, but she'd shake her clothes out later. At least now the bunnyfly was relatively safe.

Aubrie Dionne

Jumping back onto Windracer, Star cradled the bunnyfly along with her pack bag. Within a blink, they set off again on the dirt path leading to Ravencliff. She hadn't noticed until now, but her heart thudded like a violent drum, blood pounding in her head and flushing her cheeks. She was lucky. She shouldn't have ventured off course. It was only her third year as a messenger and she'd grown arrogant, assuming she could dismount and waltz around unguarded with no repercussions. Overconfidence led to laziness and a false sense of immortality. She thought of the many messengers that had been carried away, never to return.

As she reprimanded herself, the hulk of Ravencliff's fortress towered over her. The footsteps of the mountain flanked the sheer edifice of ebony rock on either side, and the stone facade rose quickly from the smothering smog to claim the horizon. Balancing the letter bag and the bunnyfly, Star rode swiftly to the main gate.

Chapter 2

Nina's Pet

Star hoped the guard stationed in the watch tower recognized the messenger's symbol of two white wings embroidered across her windswept cloak. Windracer's sides heaved with labored breaths and Star did not want to waste the horse's last bit of energy circling the fortress. She'd heard stories of messengers left outside for too long—when the drawbridge finally lowered, they were nowhere to be found.

Before she had time to panic, she heard the rickety wheels lined with chains turn, and the drawbridge lowered in time for her to ride through the main gate without delay.

Windracer's hoofbeats echoed as they crossed the massive planks. No sooner did they enter than the wheels cranked again in reverse, metal on metal, and the drawbridge rose, stifling the waft of mist trailing their heels. Star reined her horse in, completing a half circle in the main court before approaching the entry guard at the first checkpoint. "Star Nightengale from Evenspark reporting, sir."

The guard scratched his stubble on his chin and ran a hand over his curly gray hair. His armor had dents and scuffs and he looked under-cared-for and overworked. He took a long moment to look up from the paperwork on his desk, scribbling in hasty strokes. Star wondered if he finished his own letter for her to carry on her way home.

After sifting through a stack of yellowed papers, he responded with a nod. "The servants' quarters at the castle are full this night. You will stay at the Overflow Tavern." He gestured with the tip of his writing quill toward the gate leading to the main city, past the front battlements.

"Thank you, sir." Star dismounted, leaving Windracer to drink from the trough. She signed numerous documents confirming her arrival and receipt of payment, thinking about her accommodations as the parchment passed her hands. She'd delivered correspondence to the Overflow

Tavern before, and though the lodging was far from opulent, the tavern was better than the servants' quarters. However, she would be farther from the prince. Star sighed in annoyance with herself. She was being impractical and she knew it.

The guard pushed forward a rather hefty bag of coins and a note for the innkeeper. She handed him the documents, taking the items in her other hand. His eyes brightened. "You don't, by any chance, have anything for a Hal Talern, do you?"

Star pursed her thin lips. This conversation followed her in both kingdoms. She saw more disappointment than satisfaction. It was as if she were the ruler of every expectation, dream and fear when, in fact, the winds of fate carried her along as a helpless pawn.

"My apologies, sir. I have not had time to sort the letters. I can assure you they will be delivered by eventide tomorrow. If I have anything for you, it will be in your hands by then."

The guard frowned but accepted her answer nonetheless. Star wondered what kind of correspondence he awaited. Her mouth did not budge, for it was against the messenger's code to inquire.

After counting the coins, Star mustered a cheery farewell as she swiftly mounted Windracer and entered the city. Even though she visited frequently, the clarity of the air never failed to surprise her, as if she'd donned spectacles for the first time. She could see down every street and alleyway until the black wall of a building or a latched gate blocked her line of sight. She read the painted signs dangling from shops meters away and was able to chart her course much easier without getting lost, and there was no clamoring of mist blowers to clog her thoughts. Perhaps Ravencliff's high walls really were the best solution.

Evenspark did not have high walls to hold back the mist. Instead, the kingdom relied on the mist blowers, giant metal contraptions surrounding the city. They never worked in perfect synchronicity and were always sputtering, in need of repair. The older machines chugged the best they could, but stray wisps of vapor always found their way through the grid, unfurling through alleyways and spreading foggy gloom.

At least Evenspark had the grid, Star reflected, a shell of intertwined metal that kept the inhabitants in and the Elyndra out. The mist could penetrate the holes in the weave work, but the Elyndra were far too big to fly through.

Ravencliff relied on the fact the mist never rose above a hundred feet. The Elyndra did not fly in open sky and so could not breach the high walls. Archers were stationed along the cliff tops, but they seldom fired. It was a gamble, but so far they'd won.

Star supposed each kingdom's methods had their own advantages, drawbacks and dangers. Both societies were caged and imprisoned within their own walls, threatened by all sides in a state of eternal siege. She wondered if there was such a place where the mist did not flow, where people were free to roam the countryside with no qualms and visit their brethren without fear of death. Adventurers called journeymen were sent out for centuries to search out places for new colonies. But none came back.

Star reached the swinging sign with a painted frothy mug and stenciled letters that read *Overflow Tavern*. The building nestled between a smithy and a local herbalist, with two narrow alleyways in between. At this hour, both shops were closed, their tattered front hangings dangling like branches of a willow tree.

She dismounted, leading Windracer to the stable hand on duty. "Make sure that she eats only the finest grains." Star flashed a piece of gold that made his eyes light up.

"Yes, my lady."

As she dropped the coin in his palm, Star caught him eyeing her parcel of letters, staring as if he looked upon a legend.

"Have you seen one?" the boy asked before Star could turn away.

"Seen what?" Star replied, although she knew just what he referred to.

"A flying monster." His eyes slanted under heavy lids, a mask of skepticism adopted from the older boys.

Star laughed lightly, trying to ease the mood. "No, I have not."

"I heard they carried someone away just the other day. A guard bet he could stand out there for twenty minutes without getting spooked."

"That's not very smart, now is it?" Star gauged the reliability of his tale. Although the story seemed farfetched, something kept her listening. His voice had a certain ring of truth. "What happened?"

"They heard him yell, just once, and then he was gone, sword and all."

Star considered his tale, turning it around in her head. She would have to inquire further when she got to the castle. That is, if she had any letters for the royalty.

"What do you suppose the flying monsters do with the people they capture?"

Star adjusted her letter bag against her side. The stable hand's question made her uncomfortable and she needed time to think of an answer.

Should she make up a fairytale to put his fears at ease or should she be honest about the harsh way of the world?

She decided the truth might keep him from doing something stupid like the guard. "What do you think an eagle does with a mouse?" She raised her brow. Although no one knew for certain what became of the stolen villagers because no bodies were ever found, she had a hunch.

The boy bit his lower lip and took a step back. "That's what I figured. My mom's been telling me they just take them away to another land. I knew she made that stuff up."

Star ruffled the hair on his head. "No one knows for certain. Just make sure you don't go to close to those walls, okay?" She spoke in a motherly tone that surprised even her. Was she that old? Some of her friends in Evenspark had already settled down and started their new families. Star was married to her career.

"Don't you worry 'bout that." The boy tossed his new coin up in the air and caught it. "I heard the mist is rising, and it will only be a matter of time before those archers would have to start shootin'." He looked more excited than worried.

"Mist rising?" Star knew the guardians of Ravencliff kept precise measurements and the fogginess hadn't moved in years.

Just then, the tavern door opened and a group of merrymakers stumbled out, singing so loud Star thought their lungs would burst. Their revelry silenced the boy, as if it reminded him of his humble place in the world. He pulled gently on Windracer's reins. "I'll make sure she has the best care."

Star let the conversation dissipate. The stable hand had a job to attend to, and she didn't want to get him in trouble. "Thank you. I appreciate it." With a wave to the stable hand, she pushed open the tavern doors.

As expected, heads turned and eyes widened as if the music hit a lull at the same time as every conversation. Despite her attempt at entering inconspicuously, Star shone like a pearl among stones. Most of her countrymen from Evenspark were paler than the black-haired, tawny people of Ravencliff, and Star was one of the brightest and most ethereal, a trait her mother claimed came from her side of the family. Not only was she exotic looking, she wore the glimmering translucent silk of the messenger's embroidered coat, marking her importance.

After the initial shock of her entrance, the people returned to their business and Star was able to seek the owner without being bothered. Everyone knew not to get in the way of a messenger. Not only were there fierce repercussions, but the carriers were trained in all manner of combat arts. Like her colleagues, Star's reactions were fast, her movements fluid and unpredictable. Despite her small stature, everyone knew to leave her be.

A broad woman with straggly chestnut hair and layers of aprons looked up quickly from a round of bubbling mugs and extended her calloused hand. "Hilda Plin. I'm the new innkeeper."

"Star Nightengale, messenger for the Interkingdom Carriers." Star ceremoniously presented the letter from the guard. She waited patiently as Hilda read it over, trying to ignore the chorus of whispers behind her. They'd let her be, but their tongues kept moving.

"Says here you're to lodge with us." Hilda clicked her teeth together in thought. Star could tell the old barmaid favored the arrangements. The royal family paid large sums for hired services. "You can stay in the honored guest room. Top of the stairs, first door on the right." Hilda pocketed the paper and looked around, taking in the stares that people shot over their shoulders. "You've had a long journey. Go on up. I'll bring you something to eat." She handed Star a rough metal key.

Star was relieved she didn't have to sit amongst all the ogling patrons. Hilda must have understood when a woman needed her privacy. Star decided she liked the tavern's new chief-barmaid. With a courteous bow, she accepted the key and ascended the crowded steps, pushing past the waves of dark faces.

Once she secured the door to her room, she opened her coat and the bunnyfly tumbled out with a small chirp. Star took a blanket off her bed and gently placed the animal in the folds of cotton fabric. She filled a cup of water from the washbasin and positioned it in front of the bunnyfly along with the last crumbs of bread.

As Star watched the animal nibble the stale morsels, she wondered again how such a sequestered, prized pet wandered into such danger. People couldn't even get past the walls, and yet a senseless bunnyfly sneaked out, undetected. She sat by it on the floor, petting its furry head until the animal fell asleep. There was only one way it could escape. The fortress must have a crack in the facade so deep it penetrated through to the inner district, or a secret tunnel. Star stored the possibility away. She would think on it later. Now she had letters to sort.

There was a woodstove by the window, along with a pile of kindling and matches. Star started a fire, the coaxed flames breathing warmth to her small room. With great anticipation, she opened her pack bag, spreading the letters out onto the floor. She knew she should rest, but the lure of the unknown was too strong to ignore. Star needed to know where her morning roving would take her. Quickly, she organized the rolls of stamped papers into piles. The streets of Ravencliff sprang up in her memory, each letter becoming a stop along the way.

There were several letters for the inhabitants of the inner district, a place where they had an excess of money to spare on such frivolities as correspondence. Most of the letters were for the royal guardsmen of the castle. They had family members in both kingdoms, their orders taking them to posts without thought of their own personal agendas. Star always felt for those away from their homes. She would deliver their letters first.

As the pile slimmed down, Star became more and more disgruntled. She possessed no letters addressed to the royal family, thus no way to visit the prince. Disappointed, she gave in to rest. The journey caught up to her, leaving her limbs sore and weary. The fire in the woodstove rose to full flames, leaving a heady, warm ambiance inviting sleepy dreams.

Hilda's boisterous knock woke Star just as she nodded off in front of the orange light. "Dinner."

Star rushed to the door, her mind still muddled by the haziness of sleep. She opened the door to see a large platter of meats and roasted potatoes, apple cider and gingerbread. Hilda had cooked a feast.

"Hilda," Star said, her voice husky with wonderment, "this is wonderful. Thank you!" Somehow, the opulence of the food made Star forget how long it had taken to arrive.

But Hilda paid her no heed. In fact, she almost tipped the tray and dropped the food right onto Star. In a swift move, Hilda fell back a step, stumbling into the narrow hallway.

Star reacted quickly, sliding her arms underneath the tray. Hilda stared wide-eyed into her room. If Star hadn't reacted quickly, she would have been wearing her dinner instead of eating it. The innkeeper seemed like a hard woman to impress, but here she was, gaping like a schoolgirl watching soldiers march in a parade.

"What's the matter?" Star wondered if she'd somehow damaged the interior of her lodgings. "Hilda, are you all right?"

"Why, I never…" Hilda mumbled. "That's Nina's pet."

It took long moments for Star to realize Hilda stared at the bunnyfly. The animal looked up from the makeshift bed with large and vacant eyes, a piece of crumb bread stuck in its whiskers. It cooed softly, a polite noise sounding like a question.

Star's memory referenced the entire catalog of names she had delivered letters to in Ravencliff, but could think of no one named Nina. The pairing was odd because someone wealthy enough to have a bunnyfly would obviously have enough money for regular correspondence. "I'm sorry, I do not know of a Nina."

Hilda's eyes never left the bunnyfly. "Nina's just what we call her here at the tavern. That animal belongs to Bellanina, the king's daughter."

"Oh." Star's thoughts raced faster than Windracer could ever carry her. Suddenly the bunnyfly didn't seem as ridiculous. "I found it on the moors. What should I do?"

"The poor thing's been missin' for three days now. The king ordered every soldier on duty to keep their eyes peeled. The promised reward is great. Why, you should deliver it to the castle first thing in the morning."

"The castle." Star tried not to smile as her heart basked in the thought. "Of course."

Chapter 3

Breach

The castle was the centerpiece of Ravencliff, like a dark cherry on a cream-frosted cake. Chipped from the onyx stone of the mountain, the walls were polished slates of ebony sprinkled with crevices of grainy gold, where black ravens pieced together their nests with hay. The marble hall towered above the other dwellings of the city. Framed by a stone fence high enough to shadow the sun in midday, it was a fortress within a fortress, the pinnacle of the city.

It was easy enough for Star to gain access. Instead of presenting the royal seal on a letter, Star reached into her shirt and displayed the glittering bunnyfly. The guards stopped chattering in mid-sentence and parted before her like sheep before a wolf, the whites of their eyes growing with newfound curiosity. The path cleared and Star encouraged Windracer on.

A guard broke the silence as Star rode past. "Where did you find it?"

"Where no one is allowed to go," Star answered over her shoulder. She was feeling a bit mischievous, holding her key to the castle in both hands.

"Where's that? The king's brewery?" another guard quipped, igniting a series of rowdy laughter.

"No." Star strode in an elegant ceremonial canter, her translucent cloak glimmering in her wake.

"Then where was the silly thing?"

Star pulled back on the reins, halting Windracer in mid-step. She turned in her saddle to face the speaker of the question. Although his tone was haughty, he was a young lad, barely graduated from the academy. Uneven stubble grew in patches on his face. "The moors."

Silence followed as if her words turned them to stone. No one laughed any longer. Star nudged Windracer back into motion and continued along the way, passing them like she strode among statues. There were no further questions. As she left the brigade, she heard one of them mumble,

"Poor Arwen, rest in peace." Star no longer wondered about the truth of the stable hand's story.

Star approached the marble hall and dismounted, leaving Windracer to rest in the shade of a Blackwood. The castle perched on the bald spot of a foothill, several feet from ground level. Here the mist was but a shady afterthought, and the sun warmed the earth and gilded the royal gardens. Star had entered the inner sanctuary, a palace reserved for Ravencliff's elite.

She walked through rows of columns. The royal emblem of Ravencliff decorated the sandstone: a single bird flying free from a high perch on a sharp crag. Secretly, Star scoffed at the symbol. The rulers had improperly attributed such an image of freedom to a fortress where the inhabitants remained locked away. Perhaps it was a distant hope, a future they strived for to no avail.

The doors to the marble hall were propped open, allowing Star to enter the main antechamber. Lined with dramatic tapestries, velvet curtains and cushioned chairs, the hall was a regal testament to Ravencliff's exquisite grandeur. Dignitaries formed circles of gregarious speech, council ambassadors strolled with servants in tow and members of the extended royal family lounged, creating a sea of voices where laughter and whispers rode the waves in tides.

Star picked her way through the mingling crowd. She had the privilege of stepping into the inner sanctuary many times before to deliver correspondence and knew exactly whom to speak to regarding the matter of the bunnyfly. A desk raised on a pedestal stood at the far end of the great hall, where the chief of acquisitions sat, smug as a judge, in a leather studded chair.

Star frowned impatiently when she saw the line. The trail of people stretched halfway across the grand room, weaving in between the columns like a snake. She had not come at the best time. Scratching the bunnyfly's head, Star took her place at the end of the line behind a scrawny man carrying a long box in the shape of a fiddle.

The man looked back at her with a cursory glance under unruly curls of chestnut locks. When he recognized her garb, he turned full around. "So, a messenger, heh?"

Star sighed. This question also followed her in both kingdoms and she was tired of answering. "That's right."

"Delivering something important to the king?"

Although his tone was playful, Star was not amused. "You could say that, yes." In her arms, she hid the bunnyfly in a blanket borrowed from the inn. She didn't need to draw more attention to herself.

"I sent a letter out a fortnight hence, you see, and I still haven't gotten a reply."

Star stifled the urge to roll her eyes. It was going to turn into one of *those* conversations. "Sir, messengers don't keep track of who sends what to whom. We merely deliver the letters that fall into our safekeeping. I can assure you letters are seldom lost or misplaced. If you haven't heard back, then the recipient hasn't written a reply."

Again she had succeeded in dissatisfying another customer. The man glowered, shifting the weight of his fiddle box to the other shoulder. "I'm just a musician searching for a decent job, you know. I've applied to the minstrels at Evenspark several times and haven't heard back."

Star knew getting into the grid was difficult, especially if one was born in the outskirts. Both cities had population surges and little housing available. He had a better chance of finding a pot of gold under a gutter.

"Perhaps you can find a job here. That's why you're in line, right?"

"Certainly. The prices of living in the inner district of either kingdom are so high nowadays, and more and more go missing from the outskirts. They just don't have the proper defenses."

These issues stood at the forefront of Star's thoughts. Every penny she saved from her messenger's stipend brought her closer to buying her parents a new home in Evenspark's inner district. It would take several more years, but at least she would sleep soundly at night knowing they were finally safe.

The line moved quicker than Star expected, and the man's turn came before she could respond further.

"Godspeed, my friend," Star said. "I pray you do get a reply from Evenspark."

"With one three-year-old and a baby on the way, let's hope so."

* * * *

It didn't take long for Star to convince the chief of acquisitions to allow entry into the inner sanctuary. Dressed in their formal clothes of office, no one wanted to carry a sloppy bunnyfly, glitter and fur shedding on everything it touched. Soon, a snobby-nosed attendant, who obviously had better things to do, escorted her down a narrow hallway.

"Right this way." The attendant sprinted ahead, leading Star through a series of rooms and great mahogany doorways. Her tired feet left cushioned imprints in a thick, floral rug lining the walkway in elegant luxury. They exited the castle and entered the inner gardens, a labyrinth of hedges surrounding an atrium at the center. Made entirely of glass, the room was a humid greenhouse, its roof covering brightly feathered birds and large palmed ferns in a verdant array. A fountain in the center gurgled lazily, the waters rippling with streams of golden fish.

"This is her favorite place to study." He gestured with his hand, encouraging Star to enter. She stepped by him as he stood by the door, impatiently waiting for her to present the animal. With one uneasy look at the attendant, Star entered the atrium. Rounding the fountain, she could hear voices above the splashing water.

"And what is the capitol of Ravencliff?" A woman questioned with an authoritative air.

A young girl responded, "This castle, of course!"

"And who rules this castle?"

A shrill squeal erupted. "Valen does!"

"No, my dear," the woman corrected. "The King of Ravencliff, your papa." She whispered something under her breath, and Star thought she heard, "Although sometimes I think you're right."

Star spotted the pair at the opposite end of the room, sitting on twisted wicker chairs on a patio, books spread out everywhere. The girl wore a pink camisole with puffy sleeves, her hair braided in intertwined ribbons. An older woman, likely the tutor, with thinning gray hair spun up in a bun, sat opposite the girl. She wore a dress rigidly buttoned all the way up to a collar, which brushed the bottom of her pointy chin.

"Ravencliff is the ultimate power in the kingdom, controlling the entire realm of humanity. Now write the word *Ravencliff* in your letters."

Princess Bellanina's wandering gaze spotted Star. In an instant, her violet eyes gleamed. "Flopsy! Oh, my dear Flopsy!" The princess rushed over to Star in a flurry of satin and lace. Star handed her the bunnyfly and the girl cradled it like a baby, twirling around in whimsical delight.

The tutor's mouth pursed in slight annoyance. The unexpected reunion overshadowed the lesson. Star knew any further teaching might be difficult for the remainder of the morning and perhaps the rest of the day. She gave the tutor a sympathetic smile, feeling a bit guilty for interrupting the princess's studies.

"Look, Madame Erlene!" the princess exclaimed. "This messenger has found Flopsy."

"Rightly she has," Madame Erlene responded, albeit not as enthusiastically as Bellanina. She rounded the fountain to meet Star. "And what do you say to the young lady?"

"Thank you, madam." Princess Bellanina curtsied, picking up the corner of her pink dress in her hand.

Star bowed in return. "My pleasure."

"Would you care to join us this morning for tea?" Madame Erlene asked Star. "Perhaps share a story of your adventures in Evenspark?"

"I'm sorry." Star looked at her heavy shoulder bag. "I cannot. I have many letters to deliver and a schedule to keep."

The tutor nodded, a practiced gesture of acquiescence. "Of course."

Star looked to the small princess and bent to meet her eyes. "Keep a close watch over Flopsy. Don't let her wander far." Despite the seriousness of her warning, she couldn't help but smile. The girl was even more adorable than the bunnyfly.

The princess put the bunnyfly down by her feet. "It's a he."

"Oh my."

Madame Erlene's mouth twitched into a smile.

Star stifled a laugh and tried to keep her voice even and professional. "Please forgive me, Your Highness."

The princess followed the bunnyfly as it chewed an exotic fern, creating a scene that would upturn the garden keeper's stomach. She called over her shoulder, "That's all right. He gets mistaken all the time."

Madame Erlene stepped toward Star. "There are a lot of misplaced identities here at Ravencliff." Before Star could ask her to elaborate, the tutor skipped ahead to tend to the princess and her pet. "Princess Bellanina, control your bunnyfly!"

The scurrying attendant escorted Star back to the main antechamber. To her dismay, he ushered her forward too fast for any close examination of the inner rooms. Nevertheless, Star peered around every corner whenever the corridor opened. The castle halls bustled with people, but none of them were Prince Valen.

Star left empty handed. Not only did she use her only ticket, but the task of delivering all of the city's letters loomed before her with no prize to be won at the other end. As Star mounted Windracer, she shuffled through her carrier's bag in resignation, picking out the letters addressed to the guards at the castle. At least she could deliver some of the letters while she was here.

The guards looked up expectantly as Star approached the main gate. Searching through the pile, Star read each name in turn, handing the letters out like they were candy.

"Bradford Diln, Raymond Rue, Ernest Myer and Lyton Maxx." Each man came beside her, showing proof of identification, and claimed his prize. When she was finished, there were still several faces turned up, a glinting hope dwindling in each man's eye. "That's it. The rest of you will have to wait until the next messenger arrives in a few days."

There was a collective sigh of disappointment Star identified with. She, herself, felt the heavy weight of dejection clinging to her spirits. But it was her own fault. Her expectations were set too high. What had she actually hoped to accomplish?

As Star rode the final steps to the main gate, she heard a resonant tenor voice call after her. "Star Nightengale, you cannot leave until I've rewarded the famous messenger who saved my sister's beloved pet."

She realized the guards around her stared. Each one straightened a bit taller and the commotion died to silence. Some dashed back to their posts as if she'd caught them loitering.

Star whirled around in her saddle to address the speaker. Valen sat atop a black stallion, his riding cloak fluttering in the gentle breeze. He wore a rough leather tunic that hugged the rounded, smooth muscles of his chest. His face was flushed with exertion as if he'd been involved in sword practice when news came of the bunnyfly's astonishing savior.

She blinked to make sure he wasn't a dream. When she opened her eyes and the prince remained, her heart fluttered and sped. Star wondered why the fate of a pet was important enough to warrant an audience with a prince. Fumbling with the reins, her thoughts stuttered as she searched for an appropriate response. Relief flowed over her when her lips found the correct words. "I seek no reward, Your Highness. I'm merely doing my duty."

The prince gently urged his horse forward and rode up beside her. His voice fell from a full-fledged projection to a conversational tone. "I believe this is above and beyond your duty. You've made my sister happy again, which is not an easy task, and I express my deepest appreciation."

His eyes met her own as if he were shifting through the layers of her job, her duty, to study the soul that lay beneath. Star met his gaze, asking him to find what he sought. It was a bizarre occurrence, having what she wanted handed to her on a platter. Some ironic turn of fate had gleaned amusement by honoring her request. Confronted by her imaginings turning into reality, Star had no idea what to do.

The prince looked away as if he had forgotten himself. He dug into the folds of his cloak and brought out a small, glided box. Extending his arm, he handed it to her. "Here, a token of my gratitude."

Star took the box, her slender fingers brushing against his. Somehow, all of the exchanges she'd dreamed of were no longer at her disposal.

Her head was as empty as the bunnyfly's. "Thank you." Star cursed her diminishing vocabulary.

She thought the exchange had run its course, but the prince made no move to leave. "Can I have a moment of your time?"

Star was already hours behind schedule. She suspected she might have to ride out a day later than usual. Not only did she have a bag full of undelivered letters, but she'd spent the entire morning returning a bunnyfly of all things. Zetta would certainly not approve.

But there was no other answer she could give. "Most definitely." Star closed and secured her carrier's pack.

Valen smiled, appeased. "Come, let us ride."

Leaving the vicinity of the guards, Star followed the prince down a grassy slope and into the privacy of the gardens. Windracer picked her way through a bed of blooming hyacinths, their voluptuous petals emanating an intoxicating scent in the air. The moment was surreal, wrapping around her heart and squeezing it until it swelled.

Once they were out of earshot, Valen turned to Star and broke the silence. "The disappearance of the bunnyfly unsettles me. Perhaps, seeing you were the one to find my sister's pet, you can shed light where there is none."

Star leaned forward. The overhanging branches cast dappled patches of shade on his face, making his expression difficult to interpret. "Anything I can do, Your Highness."

"Please, call me Valen."

"Prince Valen." Star enjoyed saying his name.

"No, just Valen."

Star laughed lightly. "I'm sorry, I cannot address you so informally. Prince Valen will have to do."

The prince relented. "Rightly so. I heard you found the animal in the moors, outside the strong keep."

"Yes."

"And it was alone."

"Yes."

"Was there anything alongside it, any clue as to who put it there?"

"No, Your Highness. It huddled in the middle of the moors with no food, no shelter and no one to look after it."

"What type of cruel person would steal such an innocent, inconsequential creature and toss it to certain death? You'd think if they had a tiff with the royal family, they would come directly to me or my father. But instead they insist on terrorizing the pet of a little girl."

"Prince Valen, I don't believe anyone stole your sister's pet."

The prince crinkled his brow. "Then how do you suppose it got there?"

Star chose her words carefully. "Forgive me, sir, for my boldness, but have you considered the possibility your fortress has a breach?"

"A breach? What do you mean?"

"A hole in the wall. Wide enough, at least, for a bunnyfly. Maybe bigger."

Valen looked like he'd seen an Elyndra fly right out of the sky. The color drained from his face. "Impossible. This fortress is as sturdy as the mountain itself. Nothing can enter or leave without the king's permission."

"I understand your faith and your pride, but what if I am right? The castle may be in danger. The tunnel must stem from the inner rooms itself, leading into hostile territory." Star felt guilty delivering such dire tidings. It seemed to be her lot in life. "Look, I may be wrong. In fact, let us hope I am. But what if I'm not?"

"Yes, yes." The prince massaged his chin with his fingers.

"I would check on it."

He looked back at her with a glint in his dark eyes. "I don't suppose you will be staying long? I need a rider swift enough to scout the outside perimeter."

Star weighed the amount of money an assignment at Ravencliff would provide against her message carrying. Although it would probably be worth three or four runs, it was only one assignment, and her carrier job was insured indeterminably. It would put years of steady work in jeopardy. Despite the fact that her heart desired it, her brain reasoned not. "No, I must get back to Evenspark. My job depends on it."

"Of course." Valen nodded as if he understood, although his eyes fell momentarily to the knotted reins in his strong hands.

Star wondered why he seemed so disappointed by her refusal. She searched for anything she could do to help him. Her word was the only assurance she could give. "This information is safe with me."

The prince smiled oddly, as if fate teased him. "Somehow I know I can trust you. It's almost as if..."

"As if what?" Star had to know.

Valen shook off his last words as if they were meaningless. "Where did you say you grew up?"

The change in conversation startled Star. "I didn't."

"That's right. Forgive my digression."

"That's all right." Star had nothing to hide, although her origins were meager. "I live in Evenspark in the outer districts, on the border of the outskirts."

"How unfortunate." Valen seemed surprised. "But look how much you've accomplished. You're a rider of Evenspark, in fact, the head rider of the Interkingdom Carriers. I do read up on Evenspark's current events, you know."

Star blushed despite her poise. "My advancements took a lot of hard work."

"And talent, I presume."

She beamed from the inside out. It was one of those precious moments when someone recognized her for who she truly was and all she had achieved in her life above her job of delivering letters. And it wasn't just anyone—it was Prince Valen.

Star shifted in her saddle, a bit restless. She didn't know where this conversation was going, but she didn't want it to end. Unfortunately, she could think of nothing further to say.

Valen beat her to the next words. "Thank you again."

"You're most welcome."

"I'm sure you must be on your way, with all those letters to deliver."

Star knew enough to let things be and urged Windracer to start moving. "Yes, I should."

But the prince moved with her, steering his own stallion to match Windracer's gait. "You will be coming back, I presume."

"Most definitely."

"Then I look forward to our next conversation." The prince bowed in his saddle. "Until next time, Miss Star Nightengale."

"I bid you farewell, Prince Valen."

The prince rode off in a swift flurry of flowers and leaves, leaving Star to reflect on the odd conversation. She watched his scarlet cape flutter in the wake of his black stallion, turning over their words. Each sentiment was a luscious morsel, still lingering on the tip of her tongue.

Chapter 4

Father's Shadow

The rest of the day whizzed by in a blur of letters, a surge of pleased recipients and a slew of strategically planned destinations. Star made up time by scavenging cheap merchant food stands in between stops and hastily stuffing her mouth as she rode to the next delivery. Thank goodness she'd placed each letter in order the previous night, thus was able to accomplish more than one delivery at a single stop. She caught up with her deliveries when the moon reigned in the sky and the lanterns blazed like giant fireflies, one by one.

As she approached the Overflow Tavern, Star reached down to skim the bottom of her carrier's bag. She had a nagging doubt she'd overlooked a letter in the rush. Her fingers brushed wads of crumpled receipts and the crust of the bread she'd nibbled for lunch. Digging deeper, Star felt a fold in the leather where her arm had clutched the bag too tight, crinkling the corner. The weight of the letters had wedged a small piece of paper underneath the crease.

When Star brought it out into the light, her stomach pitched. Not only was it another letter, but it was the exact one Zetta had so carefully entrusted to her safekeeping. She'd been catching up all day and the outskirts were not part of her ordinary circuit. In all the commotion, she'd overlooked the most important correspondence of her job.

If she waited until morning, Star would have to delay her ride home by another day. Zetta would fume when she returned, her cheeks red as the Devil and her mouth full of questions. Star would be forced to explain the matter of the bunnyfly and why the most important letter arrived late.

She bit her lower lip. She could already hear Zetta's shriek of a voice: *You risked your life and the letters? For a bunnyfly?* And then, at an even higher pitch: *You delivered the bunnyfly before the letters? You delivered the most important letter last?*

No, it would be better if she could finish the task before sunrise. Feeling foolish and irresponsible, Star pulled on the reins and Windracer swiftly turned around, fast as the dovetail of an arrow. Star smiled at her horse's resilience to fatigue. At least this delivery would not take long.

The outskirts were an extension of the mountain behind the city, where a plate of granite hovered over a crevice between the earth and the mountain itself. It was known for sudden cave-ins and never saw the light of day. The dirt-paved streets harbored petty thieves and frantic citizens too poor to afford a residence in the inner districts. The growing population had pushed several housing communities beyond their limits, forcing many toward desperation, scrounging for food and shelter.

Star could only wonder how someone from such meager means could afford a personal message, and why he wouldn't spend the money on a way to better his makeshift accommodations.

Perhaps this message did just that.

When Star reached the outskirts, the sky was a sheet of black, and the cave was even darker still. Here, no lanterns lit the throughways. People carried their own lights, as if each of them held a piece of the sun over their shoulder to remind themselves darkness was not everlasting.

Tonight the streets were empty of golden orbs. The inhabitants had retreated long ago to their shacks thrown together with stray wood and decorated by tattered curtains. The streets were shadowy and Star did not have a lantern. Reaching in her coat pocket, she brought out a crumpled box of matches. After striking one between her fingers, she crossed the threshold and the canopy of rock hovered over her like a storm cloud.

The dwelling she sought was part of a shantytown of pillaged wood houses huddled against the backdrop of the far side appropriately titled Rugged Ridge. The number of the address was 11678.

Star peered through the darkness. A scuttling sound came from deep within an alleyway. It could be as innocent as a tomcat or as malicious as a starving vagabond. Her match fizzled out. Not wanting to draw attention to herself, she urged Windracer on in the darkness. Her horse's ability to see ahead did not concern Star. Windracer had excellent night vision and Star had trained her with frequent night walks in the misty, dimly lit streets of Evenspark.

To her dismay, the sound tracked Star through the grimy streets. Every few steps Windracer took, the scurrying followed like a delayed echo. Star looked back, but bundled trash clogged the alley.

Star cursed under her breath then dismounted Windracer, silent as a windless day. Bending down, she unsheathed a dagger lodged in the top of her boot. Every messenger had their own defenses.

A forced silence prevailed, broken only by the skittering of rats in the corner of the back alley. Holding the dagger in front of her, Star tiptoed around Windracer. As she entered the passageway, the darkness engulfed her in a stifling, black embrace.

The attack came swiftly, the thief bolting from the shadows. He knocked her to the ground, but she recovered, hoisting herself up on her elbows. Wrestling her attacker, she managed to squirm from underneath him and kicked the scraggly man in the stomach. In two seconds, she had him pinned down with her dagger hovering above his throat. "How dare you attack a messenger."

Star could barely make out the shape of a young man's face underneath his wiry brown hair. The dim light from an upper window shone further down the way and she dragged him underneath it to identify him. He looked impoverished, skinny as a lamppost, with pock-marked skin and watery eyes. The recent scar boiling above the bridge of his nose looked infected. As much as he repulsed her and set back her delivery, a rush of sympathy swelled in her heart for the vagrant.

"Messenger, heh? Well, I've got a message for you." The man wiggled and she pressed the dagger closer until the cool metal of the blade touched his skin. He stopped moving, but his eyes were still wild. "Deliver all the messages you want on that high horse of yours, collect everyone's money 'til you're richer than the king himself, but none of it will save you when they come." The man smirked, displaying a mouth full of broken, yellow teeth.

Star paused. The man must be delirious, but she had to ask. "Who? Who is coming?"

The man laughed, first quietly to himself before erupting into a full belly rumble, his ragged voice echoing out into the night.

Star let him go, disgusted. The street urchin slunk into the darkness without further quarreling, but his comment left a mark on her composure, a stain of doubt that her life was not as perfect as she imagined it to be.

She was grateful to see Windracer's familiar silhouette against the backdrop of the alley. As trained, the mare remained stationed where she left her. "Come on, girl, we have a letter to deliver."

Star remounted and continued her search. The farther she went into the outskirts, the dimmer the streets became. Not only were they severely deprived of light, but grunge and debris blocked whatever warm glow trickled from the crude windows of the inner dwellings. Star struck another match, taking note of how many she had left. This time she didn't care whom she summoned from the bowels of the underworld. Her sole purpose was to get the letter delivered in order to return home.

Number 11678 rested in the corner, behind a heap of fallen rubble. Star dismounted and struck yet another flame, throwing the previous matchstick on the littered ground below. She picked a haphazard path through the ruins, careful not to tread on a shard of broken glass or upturned scrap metal. After a swift knock, she waited at the sloped entrance.

The door opened and a young man emerged, his face illuminated by the flickering of the matchstick. He wore only a pair of black leather pants, his upper body naked, exposing sinuous muscles covered in painted tattoos. A herd of racing horses ran down his arm in blue-black ink. Star had to keep her head up and remind herself not to stare at the elaborate decorations or the curves of his chest.

His chin jutted out from a strong-boned face that commanded respect. He looked like a lion waiting to pounce. He smiled at Star like he wondered whether to eat her. "Yes?"

Star did not flinch. She thought she could outwit him, if need be. "I have a message for a Fallon Leer."

The man leaned against the opened door. "That's me."

Star held her head high. With one eyebrow arched, she leveled her eyes with his own penetrating gaze. "I need to see identification."

With a furtive glance at Star, the man reached in his pocket and brought out a woven chain. Suspended on the necklace hung a metal tag glittering in the glowing embers of Star's matchstick. Sure enough, the tag read *Fallon Leer*. Star recognized the gold inscription immediately. He was a former member of Ravencliff's elite Royal Guard. Either he'd quit or they'd thrown him out.

Star didn't have the time to consider his deposition further. She dutifully brought out the letter. "It is my job to warn you there is no return address. Open it with discretion."

Fallon Leer laughed lightly, his voice smooth as aged wine. "I know who it's from, thank you."

Star turned around, but the man grabbed her hand with his own callused fingertips, his skin rough and hot to her touch. For a moment she thought she would have to test her combat skills once again, but he released her. "Wait." He disappeared inside the darkness of his shambled quarters before emerging with another letter. "This goes directly to Zetta."

Star froze at the mention of her superior's name. Why would a scoundrel like him know Zetta? But under the terms of her messenger code, her lips remained sealed like the secret letter he held in his hands.

"And the payment?"

"To be paid by the recipient."

She considered his request, weighing the unlikely possibility Zetta would pay for any letter from him. But it wasn't in her authority to inquire. If Zetta refused to pay for it, the letter would be shredded and discarded. She could not bend the rule of the Interkingdom Carriers. Taking it from his hands, Star slipped the letter into her carrier bag and turned away.

He called after her, a comical lilt to his tone. "It's a little late for a messenger to be gallivanting around, isn't it?"

Star turned back, her hair whipping around her face in a shining veil. "I can take care of myself." His eyes flared as if he found her bold retort appealing. Feeling a little awkward, she mounted Windracer and rode away.

* * * *

When Star returned to the Overflow Tavern, most of the booths were empty. Hilda had stacked mugs in toppling array on the bar and wiped the tabletops with a rag and soapy water. Dinner had ended long ago.

"Long day?" Hilda asked as Star plopped herself down into a booth by the windowsill. She was grateful to have a warmly lit place to return to, but somehow the glow of firelight couldn't quite shake the haunting images of the night's rambles out of her head. At least her bag was empty.

"You could say that, yes."

Hilda grinned wide. "Let me get you our special tonight. It will make it all worth it. I hope you got a substantial reward for returning that bunnyfly."

The barmaid's comment reminded Star of Valen's gift. Digging in her coat, she brought the gilded box into the lantern light, and it sparkled as though a chip of the rising sun had fallen into her hands. Star immediately held it down, afraid to draw attention, as two men sauntered in from the night and sat in the booth behind her. One was older, almost her father's age, and the other was not much older than herself.

As she smoothed her fingertips over the lid, she overheard their conversation waft up from the wooden stalls.

"More and more these days, there's talk of war."

"It's a good thing that mist is holding back Evenspark's army," the younger man grumbled. "The Queen of Evenspark's been raving mad ever since our king took that silly nobody as his bride."

"Ha. He passed her up many years ago for a barmaid, a young girl, nonetheless."

"She's a nobody."

"But she's beautiful, and from what I hear, Evenspark's queen isn't exactly a swan, you know."

"What have you heard?"

The older man's voice fell to a whisper. "I heard she's got some hideous disease, skin all puckered up with pus and blood."

Star shook her head in disgust of the gossip. The rumors of Evenspark's disfigured queen had spun out of control ever since her birth. The queen was a reclusive sort, sequestering herself in the castle and only showing her veiled face at royal ceremonies. But it was no reason for Ravencliff's ruffians to create pernicious lies.

She'd had enough of their ridiculous talk and took a quick breath of air, ready to intrude when the younger man responded in exasperation. "Naw. That's only a story meant to scare tots into eating their vegetables. No one's actually seen her face. She's always wearing some veil or another."

"What with the Elyndra, you'd think they have enough scary stories for the little 'uns. No, I think there's some truth in it. Why else would she hide her face?"

Star braced herself for a fight, but the younger man brushed it off. "Suit yourself, it's a moot point anyway. He married the girl nobody and now they have Bellanina."

"Yes, but the king doesn't need another heir. Prince Valen is quite enough to keep the kingdom going."

"And dual heirs always stir up trouble."

Star hunched down. The conversation grew increasingly intriguing. If they caught her eavesdropping, their tongues would not wag any further.

"Let us hope Valen can smooth over any quarrels."

"Yeah, there's Princess Vespa, the queen's niece over in Evenspark. There are rumors Valen's betrothed to her already."

The word *betrothed* assaulted her ears and Star's heart felt like it tore into two halves. The door to her hopes slammed with a rude *thud*. She couldn't help but keep listening, like one captivated by a hunter's arrow as it rode the wind to strike a deer.

"Let's hope he doesn't mess it up like his father."

"Yeah, choose some beautiful girl nobody and make everyone angry."

Star looked at the gilded box guiltily. She couldn't possibly be the one to steal Valen's heart. Slowly, her fingernails pried open the latch and she raised the lid.

Inside laid a jeweled necklace with a ruby, bigger than her eye, chipped into the unmistakable shape of a heart.

Chapter 5

Special Delivery

A rolling mass of clouds filled the sky as Star prepared for her journey back to Evenspark. Ravencliff's crimson flags stretched taut in the wind gushing from the east. A storm brewed just beyond the mountains clustered around the city's edge. If Star was lucky, she could outrun it, but it was unlikely. She would have to deal with mist, dangerous flying beasts and torrents of rain.

Despite the urgency of the moment, Star couldn't help but feel a nonsensical urge to remain at Ravencliff. She had tossed in her sweat-drenched sheets all night, her limbs filled with agitation and her heart at odds with reason. Did she intend to take down a kingdom with an infatuation? Actually, the best thing she could do was stay far away from Valen and let fate spin its course unhindered.

After stuffing the last batch of outgoing letters into her carrier bag, Star mounted Windracer and turned to the lead guard on duty. "Throw down the drawbridge. I am ready to depart."

Draft horses, as tough as dragons, heaved and the wheels of the gate turned. The metal chains clinked, slowly at first then increasing speed until a rhythmic percussion of chinks filled the air. Star felt Windracer gearing up, her front hoof stomping the ground in anticipation.

Then a horn blew, wailing like the complaint of a suffering banshee. A guard calmed the horses and the wheels rumbled to a halt. The drawbridge hovered in midair, a slim crack between wood and stone revealing a misted slate of endless pewter. Frustrated, Star turned around in her saddle.

The cause of the delay appeared to be a hooded figure riding a stallion. The horse dashed toward her, past the guards of the courtyard, stirring up dust in its wake.

Star's anger caught fire. Not only was the rider interfering with her schedule, but he also put her at odds with the upcoming storm. She needed to get back as soon as possible. She had worked hard to catch up all day yesterday, and now here was one person wanting to delay everyone's letters and Star's duty.

In the turbulence of the ride, with the wind whipping against the rider, the hood fell free. Star recognized Valen and her irritation fizzled. Closing the last few paces, he rode up beside her. "My apologies, Miss Nightengale." The prince looked like he hadn't slept well either. Dark circles framed his keen blue eyes, and his wavy hair jutted out at all angles. "I have one more letter for you to deliver."

She didn't want to create a scene in front of the guards or put him in any questionable circumstances where people would gossip about them. She wondered if he had contrived some fake letter just to see her again. A part of her hoped, but another part dreaded. She had no desire to sunder relations between the two kingdoms. "You could have waited. The next messenger rides out today."

"No." He shook his head as if to drive phantoms out of his thoughts. "This could not wait."

Star took the letter in her hands, her fingers clumsily brushing his. She couldn't help but read to whom it was addressed. He'd hastily scribbled *Evenspark Castle, Princess Vespa* on the front.

Her thoughts reeled, turned upside down. Perhaps she had misread his every move. Perhaps, to him, she was only a messenger, delivering a love letter to the correct recipient. How could she have been so stupid?

Her eyes welled with unwanted tears and she turned away to hide her embarrassment. "I'll make sure she receives it." Her lips tightened.

The prince pulled her back, forcing her to look into his eyes. His breath fell on her lips. "You make your own destiny."

Not knowing what his words meant, Star yanked Windracer's harness and turned away.

"Guard, I'm ready. Lower the gate." The guard turned to Valen, since he'd signaled the initial halt.

Valen waved. "Yes, let the bridge down. Let her go."

The lowering of the drawbridge passed in awkward silence. For Star, it seemed like an eternity. The moment the wood touched ground, she whipped the reins and burst into motion, leaving without another word. Even though she told herself not to, as she crossed the drawbridge, she couldn't help but look back. The prince stood where she had left him, his hand rising in silent farewell.

Star's thoughts boiled into turmoil and the misted countryside held no distraction. Fate's cruel irony laughed in her face as she held the letter

Aubrie Dionne

addressed to Princess Vespa in her carrier bag. She would deliver it, of course. It was her duty. But she didn't have to relish the task.

Suddenly, a giant flutter and a gust of wind soared above her head. Star looked up just in time to see the mist curl around a set of black spidery legs. She tried to calm her heart as it sprinted ahead, skipping a few beats. The beast would have to time the arc of its descent precisely when Windracer would pass underneath.

Star crouched in her saddle, searching the tendrils of mist hovering over her. As if drawing on Star's growing fear, Windracer quickened her pace. Star wondered how long her horse would be able to keep up the faster gait, and if the Elyndra could calculate its plunge once again with the change of speed in mind. Slowly, careful not to fall out of her saddle, Star reached behind her and unsheathed her dagger. Next time, she would be ready for the attack.

Sure enough, several heartbeats later, the rush of air came again. Star ducked in the saddle, raising her arm with the dagger in hand. She felt a thorny appendage scratch her forearm, groping at her. Star thrust the dagger upward, but was not able to reach high enough to stab the belly of the beast. The Elyndra flew away again, empty-handed.

Star held her wounded arm like it was a baby, rubbing it with her other hand. It was fortunate that her cloak had long sleeves. The fabric was torn in a gash, ripping down the length of her arm.

She twisted the reins around her arm in several loops. Next, she dug her feet deeper into the stirrups, locking them in place. If the beast attempted to pick her up, then it would have to carry her horse as well, and she didn't think it could manage the extra burden.

Star sheathed the dagger. The blade reached too short to cause any damage and the iridescent carapace covering the Elyndra's legs was too thick to penetrate. She would have to think of another tactic.

But she did not have enough time before it attacked again. Star's initial shock gave way to blazing fury, and this time she grabbed one of its spindly legs. She yanked down and twisted, throwing it off balance. The beast careened backward into the mist. She had caught it off guard. Behind her, she heard it tumble onto the ground.

Star did not look back to see what became of the beast. It did not attack again, but she could not subdue her racing heart. It beat against her chest like a wild animal held against its will in the cage of her ribs. Her stomach pitched, and she was thankful she hadn't eaten anything after Hilda's beefy breakfast.

It had been Star's first physical contact with the flying beasts. The Elyndra had always been a ghost of a threat, a legend spun by the fireside to scare wild children into behaving. Mothers would say, "Eat your dinner, or I'll let the Elyndra carry you away to the bad children's land." Sometimes Star even wondered if they were out there at all or if it was a myth created by past queens in order to control their subjects.

Now she knew the Elyndra were real, and Zetta's warnings rang with the bell of truth resonating in her head.

The remaining stretch of the journey was a blur of scattered thoughts and anxious fretting. Relief came when the metal grid work surrounding Evenspark claimed the horizon in a shell of wires capping the hilltop. Blacksmiths had forged the giant screen a century ago, welding it together and attaching it to a large gate that looked like a mouth of crooked dragon's teeth.

The screech of the grid coming apart was like angels singing to Star's ear. She rode through the mouth of metalwork and, for the first time, looked back to make sure it closed behind her. Star watched mesmerized as the chrome strands intertwined once again, sealing the Elyndra out. The grid had never been more reassuring and relief eased her tired muscles, despite the fact that she carried Valen's letter to Vespa.

Taking deep breaths to calm herself, she and Windracer trotted toward headquarters.

"Something wrong?"

Star jumped in her saddle. Immersed in her thoughts, she didn't see Zetta approach. Did the woman look for her arrival day and night? "Zetta," she said, breathless, "I was attacked."

"Attacked!" Zetta's voice rose into a high-pitched squeal. She scrambled the final few steps to meet Star.

"Yes." Star dismounted. "An Elyndra came for me." She showed Zetta the torn sleeve of her cloak.

"And the letters?"

Star took a quick intake of breath. The fact Zetta cared more for the letters than her health shocked her. Her tone was cold as evening's chill. "All delivered by last night's eventide."

Zetta swayed, falling back in a wash of relief. "I thought the Elyndra weren't fast enough to catch you."

"Me too. Either they're getting quicker or they're getting smarter." Star couldn't decide which was more frightening.

"And have you brought the letters from Ravencliff?"

"Yes, I have." Star swished her cloak around her shoulder, revealing the swelled carrier's bag.

"Good. I'll take the bag to the first checkpoint and have the letters processed."

At the time, Star didn't think much of it when she relinquished the letter bag to Zetta. With the aftermath of the attack still fraying her nerves, she'd forgotten Fallon Leer's letter to her superior.

Zetta put her palm on Star's forehead. "You look peaked. Go to the Carriers Station and rest. I'll get the letters back to you once they are processed. Chloe, over there, can take Windracer to the stables. In the meantime, I'll fetch a healer to look you over."

"Thank you, Zetta." Maybe the old crone cared for her after all.

Chapter 6

Replacement

There was further upheaval waiting for Star once she reached the Carriers Station. As she entered the large domed hall, it seemed as if every duty guard stared at her. Zetta hovered at the edge of the grid, most likely processing the new set of letters. She probably hadn't even dispatched the healer yet.

Star took a seat on the first available bench by the door, ignoring the apprehensive glances, and buried her head in her hands. With her eyes shut, she rubbed the temples of her forehead, trying to make sense of all the commotion and the raging emotions overwhelming her senses.

When she finally did look up, the guards still shot glances at her over their shoulders. Star weaved a hand through her translucent hair then smoothed her cloak, making sure it was tied straight. Did she look disheveled?

The atmosphere of the usually bustling room was tentative and hushed. People crept back and forth, silently performing their daily duties. No errant conversations were struck up and no easy laughs or wayward smiles were exchanged.

Star looked around, baffled. Had someone died during her absence? She was even more aggravated when no one made an effort to debrief her.

Journey-worn and weary, Star approached the head collector at the main desk. She recognized his curly hair, white as sea foam, from previous runs. He had always been kind to her and she knew she could trust him. "Hello, Darmond."

The old man raised his head from his littered desk and nodded. "Miss Nightengale, it's good to see you returned safely." He returned to shuffling his papers.

"Thank you, Darmond." At this point, Star had no patience for congenial matters. She bent over the desk, meeting him eye to eye, and spoke in a whisper. "Has something changed since I was gone?"

The papers froze. Darmond squinted. "What do you mean?"

Star bent even closer, her cloak brushing some of the letters piled on his desk. "Darmond, why is everyone staring at me?"

Darmond sighed heavily and looked around with suspicious eyes. Star could tell he tread a fine boundary between his job and the desire to help her.

"Darmond, please, I must know."

"Zetta hasn't told you?"

"No. We had other urgent matters to discuss."

Darmond sniffed, rubbing his nose as if the conversation made him nervous. "It seems while you were away, you've been replaced." His face crinkled in apology, the wrinkles crisscrossing around the corners of his eyes.

"Replaced? What do you mean?" Star's voice gained force although she knew this type of uproar was the exact mania Darmond tried to avoid. Still, *replaced* was simply not a word Star was familiar with and certainly not what she expected.

Darmond winced. "There's a new head of Interkingdom Carriers. The guards, they are waiting to see if you make a scene."

"What?" Star whipped around, her cloak fluttering. The wall of letterboxes stood by the doorway where she had entered. They contained direct assignments from Zetta to the messengers. With all of the mayhem scrambling around in her mind, she'd strolled directly by it without checking. Star tramped across the room. She didn't care who saw her or what the others thought. She just wanted to know the truth.

Sure enough, someone had stenciled another name on Star's letterbox. Star smoothed her fingers along the newly carved wooden plaque. "Tia Rood?"

Whispers filled the air behind her. Star could feel multiple gazes searing her back.

A person with a strong voice called over her shoulder. "Excuse me, young lady. Can I help you with something?" It sounded more like a command than a question.

Star whirled around to see a large-boned woman towering over her. She had short graying hair and small blue eyes that could pierce steel. The woman tilted her pointed chin down to gaze upon Star with arrogant supremacy.

"My letterbox. It's not here."

"What's your name?" The woman's tone dripped with condescension.

"No, you don't understand, it used to be—"

"What's your name?" the woman asked again, relentless and unsympathetic.

"Star Nightengale."

"I see." Her eyes slanted. "Your box has changed. It's down over there in the corner, bottom slot."

The woman turned to leave, but Star summoned enough courage to keep her still. "Wait. The top spot is supposed to be my box. I am the head rider of the Interkingdom Carriers." Star's words came across as more aggressive than she'd intended. "And who are you?"

The woman's eyebrows rose like she'd seen an annoying gnat fly before her and wanted to squish it. "Zetta has named a new head rider. That would be me, child. Tia Rood." With that, the woman turned and marched away, leaving Star to gape in numbed astonishment.

Her immobility didn't last long. Collecting the remnants of her pride, Star ignored the staring guards and burst through the doors of the Carriers Station. She would not give up so easily.

Star set off at a sprint, her thoughts spiraling around the name Tia Rood. Betrayal tore through her emotions; not only by Zetta but by the entire system she once believed was just. She had a thousand accusations, all bubbling, brewing and threatening to explode. It took all of her self-control to hold her composure together as she tried to form coherent arguments she knew Zetta had no validation against.

Zetta was exactly where Star thought she would be—hovering over the collectors as they screened the new shipment of letters. She looked up distractedly as Star approached. "You're supposed to be resting, Star. I've just sent the healer."

But Star was in no mood for orders. "Zetta," she said, holding her voice within the confines of agreeable conversation, "who is Tia Rood and why is she named head rider?"

Everyone, including the head collector, looked up in sheer astonishment. Zetta stopped shuffling the letters and gestured for Star to meet her beyond the ears of the other workers. They walked away from the collectors toward the clang of the mist blowers. Star could barely contain her emotions as she waited for Zetta to answer her question.

"Dear Star, you know I must do what is in the best interest of the Interkingdom Carriers." Zetta's words were practiced and unemotional.

"But I've trained all my life. I'm the best rider you have."

"Tia Rood comes from a background of great expertise. She's worked at the castle for years now and understands what it is to be diplomatic."

"With all due respect, diplomacy has nothing to do with riding—"

"Star, we need someone with years of experience in charge. Someone who can navigate sticky situations with grace and ease. Someone who will be respected by all."

She knew she was less than smooth when dealing with patrons. Sometimes her desire for quality and efficiency put her at odds with other people's wishes, and her curtness when asked about the letters didn't help. But she had always thought the decisions she made were fair.

Whatever the reason, it didn't matter. To Zetta, Tia was either some great letter goddess or an age-old friend. Star became more and more frustrated with every word from Zetta's mouth. The barrier separating thought from speech dissolved, leaving Star with no filter to hold back her words. In a rash moment, she spoke her mind. "Zetta, that woman is way too big to ride. She'll never make it to Ravencliff." Guilt shot through her for saying it, but the comment had already been spoken and there was no way to take it back.

"Enough!" Zetta's words silenced Star's complaints for good. "You have overstepped your position here. If I wanted your opinion, I would have asked for it. Tia will finish your mission for today. Collect your empty letter bag and go home. I am assigning you a period of house arrest as you heal from the mental strain your being attacked has caused."

Zetta's command shocked Star out of her wits. She felt aggravated, cheated and, above all, embarrassed. Not only had she reacted unprofessionally, but she had fueled the fires of hate, making the situation even worse. Gathering her letter bag, she skulked away in silent resignation. Her one consolation was the fact she didn't have to deliver that awful love letter to Princess Vespa.

Darmond stopped her before she crossed the threshold into town. "Wait! Stop, Miss Nightengale, immediately!"

Both Star and Zetta looked at him like he had lost his good reason, but the head collector stood confidently, a single letter in hand. "This letter requests Star Nightengale to deliver it with her own hands and no one else."

"What?" Zetta ran over before Star could say a word, letter in hand to inspect it herself. Star wondered who would choose her as their single delivery messenger.

Zetta held the letter up to her eyes as if Darmond had misread it. She crinkled her nose in disgust and handed Star the sealed paper. "Fine, you may deliver this one. But afterward, go right on home and rest." Her eyes grew watery with melancholy, but Star knew it was all a bunch of wonderful nonsense by now. "We care for your well being here at Evenspark's Interkingdom Carriers."

Star thought she'd won a small victory. At least one of her customers had the common sense to stand by her. As she took the letter in her own hands, she looked down to see who would exhibit such an ostentatious show of favoritism.

A surge of irrepressible heartsickness came over her as she beheld the revolting truth of the recipient of the letter. A hasty scribbled name mocked her sore emotions: *Princess Vespa.*

Chapter 7

Evenspark Castle

Unlike the slick ebony walls of Ravencliff, Castle Evenspark glittered like it was studded with millions of diamonds. Made entirely from granite embedded with mica, the glinting silver chips refracted the rays of the sun, casting multifaceted prisms in every direction. In the height of the afternoon, it sparkled beneath the grid.

But not for Star. Riding past the glimmering facade, Star was too immersed in her own thoughts to appreciate the splendor. She couldn't imagine what cruel, twisted inclination made Valen request her as the specific liaison of his love letter to Princess Vespa. Was he blind to her feelings? Had she completely masked her blossoming infatuation? Or was he purposefully confirming whom he truly loved in an effort to push the cravings of her meager heart away?

At this point, Star reasoned, any more thought spent on her relationship to Valen was wasteful. Prince Valen loved Princess Vespa, and the world would be at peace. The two of them even possessed the same initials. One couldn't argue predestined perfection.

"Wait here, Windracer, I'll be right back." Star dismounted, tying Windracer to a fence post and marched the remaining steps to the main antechamber as if she paced the final steps to her doom. She presented the letter to each guard and an attendant ushered her to the princess's room without further delay. Even the guards, eager and willing to escort her, seemed to know whom the letter was from.

The highest tower held Princess Vespa's room, overlooking the sprawling city of Evenspark in a grand balcony carved from granite and marble, flanked by giant stone dragons. The statues eternally launched into flight, their wings spread like they would come to life at any moment and flutter off with a breathless whim.

Star found the princess standing on her balcony, the wind whipping her auburn hair and satin shawl in one single rush of crimson and lace as she gazed upon her subjects, watching their lives from afar.

Vespa was everything Star was not. Star glimmered in ethereal moonlight and Vespa flaunted vibrant, earthy colors and had emerald eyes, rosy cheeks, cherry lips, and hair the deep hue of sunset. Her mother was the queen's sister, linking her ever so closely to the ruling throne. Princess Vespa's ancestors dated all the way back to Evenspark's first rulers and her father was a nobleman from Ravencliff. The two strains of opposite genes blended in perfect union to create the most beautiful woman in all the land.

Vespa turned around and the room brightened, her eyes casting joy like a spell. "Finally, my long-awaited letter has arrived."

Star bowed, presenting the document silently. Like a slaughtered opponent, she had absolutely nothing to say.

The princess took the parchment in her smooth, silken hands and tore the seal immediately. Star turned to leave, but Vespa said, "Messenger, you must stay. I will have a reply sent immediately."

Star couldn't bear to stand there while Valen's delicate words were read. "I apologize, Your Highness, but I have other duties to attend to."

Vespa's arms dropped to her sides, the letter half opened. Her eyes suddenly burned like a forest set on fire. "What duty is greater than serving your beloved princess?"

Star paused, not knowing how to respond to such audacity. She stifled an inappropriate remark. "My apologies, Highness."

Her words seemed to appease Vespa. The princess sat on her velvet chaise, raising her slippered feet onto an embroidered cushion. The letter drew back her attention. She unfolded the parchment with relish and her lips curved into a luxurious smile.

As the princess read, Star stood awkwardly in the foyer. Although her body ached from the journey and every muscle in her legs threatened to give out, she knew sitting was unacceptable unless invited. It didn't look like Vespa was going to offer any kind of hospitality.

Instead of watching Vespa's pretty face interpret the letter, Star looked around the princess's room, her eyes falling on jeweled necklaces, silver mirrors and feathered hairpieces. She saw chiffon shawls and lace blouses, gold barrettes and strung pearls. The princess had it all, and Valen as well.

Then, all of a sudden, Vespa cried out as if an Elyndra had flown right onto her private balcony. The shrill, harsh utterance was hardly a word at all but more of a guttural reaction. Star looked back at her in shock. "What is the matter, Princess?"

Vespa clutched the letter so hard it wrinkled in her hands. She stared at the writing like the loopy circles spelled out a curse.

Star couldn't help but ask in a hushed whisper, "What did he say?"

The princess's squinty eyes simmered. Her voice grew low and threatening. "How dare you ask about my personal letters! Get out!"

Star had overstepped her boundaries as a message carrier. Zetta told her never to get invested in the lives of the recipients and now, because of Valen, she'd gotten involved in the highest sense. She stood before the raging princess like a dumb donkey, trying to make sense of her words or the intent of the letter.

"Get. Out." The princess pronounced each syllable clearly as if Star was slow of hearing. She pulled on a braided cord and a bell rang, echoing into the hall. "If you don't remove yourself, I'll have someone remove you."

Regaining her composure, Star bowed and left immediately. As she strode across the length of the room, two maidservants ran past her like scurrying mice, shouting, "What is it, Your Highness?" and "How can we help?"

Star exited the room but lingered in the corridor, listening closely as Vespa poured her heart out to her lackeys. "It's Prince Valen," she said, her voice twisted in anguish. "He wants to call off the betrothal."

Star fell back to the stone wall, stunned. Valen's words came back to her with a newfound meaning. *You make your own destiny.*

"Did he say why?" one of the cowering maidservants asked, probably more out of curiosity than concern for Vespa's wellbeing.

Star held her breath. If Valen mentioned anything concerning a messenger, the princess would have her thrown in the dungeon as a traitor. She would never deliver another letter again. Not that she had a decent job left anyway. Star pushed the thought away like an unpleasant memory. She would deal with that situation later. There was enough strife happening right now. She clenched her sweaty palms and prayed.

"No," Vespa replied. "He gave no reason whatsoever. He says that it's for the best."

The second maidservant's meager voice came next and Star had to strain her neck and lean back to hear. "But how can something dreadful like this be for the best?"

Vespa sighed. "I have no idea." Then her voice grew steely and resolute. "One thing is for sure. He's going to pay."

Star descended the spiral steps, leaving the princess to be consoled by her maidservants. Although her footsteps were slow and methodical, her mind cranked like a thousand miniature wheels all turning in different directions at the same time.

But one thought kept surfacing amidst the chaos—Valen's mysterious behavior may not have anything to do with her. He might have canceled the betrothal for a number of reasons, the least of them being some inconsequential letter carrier. The thought disappointed Star, but at the same time freed her from any guilt that somehow she stood in the way of kingdom politics, placing the entire realm in jeopardy.

As she walked back to Windracer, Star reflected on her tumultuous day, trying to piece together the fragments of stinging memories and make sense out of the chaos. Not only did she start the day by leaving Valen in a rash fit of anger, but she was attacked by a mythological flying beast, expelled from the job she'd pursued her entire life, and then was forced to deliver the one letter she would rather have burned. If the engagement hadn't been broken, then it would probably be the worst day of her entire life.

With a whiff of irony and a pang of indulgent guilt, Star realized that watching the spoiled princess's face turn sour made it all worth it.

Chapter 8

Destiny's Child

The night Valen wrote Vespa's letter was the night he remembered where he had seen Star before and why she had kept a piece of his heart all along.

Like many fond memories, it all began with a bright, sunny afternoon. The sky held endless blue and the sun blazed brilliantly, sizzling the morning mist. It was ten years ago, when Valen verged on becoming a dashing young man. Those days would always be held in his heart as the golden times of glory before the Elyndra dominated the countryside and before the tragic accident claimed his mother's life.

Valen had visited Evenspark with his parents, witnessing the Great Equestrian Tournament in which Evenspark's riders raced for trophies and acclaim. Perched in the stadium's royal viewing box as honored guests of the queen, Valen sat in front of his two parents with Princess Vespa on his right side. He looked everywhere for the mutilated face of the infamous Queen of Evenspark, but she hid behind velvet curtains in another royal viewing box. Disappointed, he settled for the race ahead and Vespa's whining.

"It is so tiresome waiting for the entrants to be assembled." Vespa pulled a strand of her auburn hair behind her ear.

"They have to check to see if their horses are ready," Valen explained in an attempt to instigate polite conversation. "If there's a pebble in a horse's hoof, it could mean losing the race by a mere few seconds."

"Hmm." Vespa didn't seem interested in the activities below. Instead, she twirled a sapphire bracelet around her slender wrist. He'd tried to win her attention several times that day only to be scorned by her haughty pride. Just sitting next to her made his blood simmer. They were supposed to be getting to know each other and she wasn't helping a smidgen.

Frustrated, Valen turned his eyes to the arena and spied the light-haired rider. She looked like she'd recently turned seventeen, the legal age for competing. He hadn't ever seen her before, and although her hair was white as winter's grasp, she was so small and so young. Her horse was a glorious, majestic beast, massive as a king's carriage and dark as a raven's wings with a thick mane of braided ebony and hoofs of polished silver. Together they were converse entities, like midnight and the moon, the horse absorbing light and the girl reflecting it as if a thousand glimmering particles dusted her hair and skin.

Valen watched in fascination as the race began. The small rider sprinted ahead of the crowd of participants. Her horse pounded the earth with an even gait, propelling them ahead with effortlessness and grace. As she rode, her diaphanous hair streamed behind her in a cascade of pure luminescence.

Vespa's whine interrupted his thoughts. "I have twenty horses just as beautiful as any of those."

"Yes, but do you know how to ride any of them?" Valen surprised himself with the venom in his voice. Vespa frayed his nerves.

"Prince Valen!" his mother whispered from behind him in his ear. "Behave yourself. We are honored guests."

Reprimanded, Valen grew silent, watching the white rider as she cleared the curve of the ring, stirring up dust behind her horse's hooves. She'd reached the final stretch. A wave of admiration for her overtook him and he had an overwhelming surge of hope that she would win.

Suddenly, as she closed the distance to the finish line, another rider, still on her second lap, turned the corner too quickly, tumbling to the ground with her horse in a tangle of limbs. The horse righted and trotted away, leaving the woman to be stampeded by the incoming riders. Valen yelled, along with the crowd, but the woman lay unconscious, oblivious to their warnings.

To everyone's surprise, the white rider turned around. In a swift change of direction, she rode to the fallen woman, jumped off of her horse and pulled her to the edge of the coliseum where healers stood ready on the sidelines.

Although greatly relieved for the woman who'd fallen, Valen had a sudden pang of disappointment for the white rider's fate. He thought for certain she'd forfeited the race. She would be a hero, but she'd forsaken her title and any chance for entry to the Interkingdom Carriers. Valen clenched his fists so tightly his knuckles turned white. He watched as the other riders rounded the bend.

In a heartbeat, the white rider jumped back on her horse. As the other riders passed, she charged forward, riding through a cloud of dust in their wake. It was impossible, Valen reasoned, that a rider starting from a standstill could overtake a mass of horses in mid-flight, but he found himself rooting for her anyway.

As if his wishes traveled through the air, the rider gained a final burst of momentum, sprinting ahead of the pack to complete the race in a glorious show of inspiration. The crowd roared as she crossed the finish line. It was a magical moment and Valen had witnessed the glory of it firsthand.

Caught up in the rider's triumph, Valen rose. His father did not notice. He was deeply involved in drinking and eating, mulling over politics with some regent from Evenspark, yet his mother glanced at him with a questioning blink.

"I will go down and congratulate the winner." He turned to leave, though he knew better. He could not entertain each whimsy that flew his way, but the rider blinded his better judgment.

His mother reached over his seat and took his arm. "Valen, you must remember your place. This is not our country, and the queen will do the honor." She pulled him aside. "Besides, you are here to spend time with Vespa. You should not leave her side."

As always, the political game of what was proper and what should be done pinned him down. He bowed to his mother then returned to his seat beside Vespa. When he searched the center of the stadium, he could not spot the rider. She had disappeared.

All throughout the day he thought of her as Vespa's voice rang incessantly in his ears and throngs of people flooded the stadium below. A slew of events followed. Valen watched the jousting with mild interest and met the princess's brigade of ladies-in-waiting as they dragged him through a tedious tour of the royal gardens. He thought the day would never end when the queen invited him to join the royal family at the Midnight Ball.

As he entered the ballroom, Valen's eyes were filled with dazzling wonders. It was impossible, despite his reluctance, not to be impressed. Fiddlers and flutes riffed ballads and jigs, and servants balanced golden trays full of amber wine underneath jeweled chandeliers. Valen marveled at diamond-studded cups, rows of roasted pheasants, and hairpieces so high they seemed to brush the lofty ceiling. Evenspark had more opulence than Ravencliff and flaunted it.

Of course he danced with Vespa all evening, stifled by her chiffon and lace. When she left to adjust her beaded updo of curls, Valen ducked away and hid behind the flowered vases. Spying through the crowd, he saw his mother chatting with other noblewomen and his father involved in a card game at the wine table. For a few moments, he would not be missed.

Skipping down the marble steps on sore feet, Valen rejoiced in his escape. He shed the baldric and scarf boasting Ravencliff's stately red and black colors, throwing the garments at the foot of the grand staircase. He walked through open glass doors to a private, walled garden where a fountain streamed water in the moonlight.

At first, he thought he spied a fairy come to dance in the beams of translucent radiance, or a beautiful ghost of the night, lingering in a place where she once sat as a young woman. Then, as he walked closer in silent steps, he recognized the white rider from the day's events. She wore a simple white gown. Tiptoeing around the base of the fountain, she seemed as if she'd broken free of the mob as well, an escapee of the roaring laughter above their heads in the ballroom.

Valen called out to her just as she turned to slip back inside. "Congratulations on winning the race today."

The girl whirled around like she'd been caught and, seeing that it was a teasing young man and not a castle official, relaxed her tensed shoulders, her hair streaming down in white waves of glittering light. "Thank you."

"That's quite a horse you've got."

She smiled as if he'd mentioned a dear friend and the muscles in her face eased. "Windracer comes from a line of the finest horses bred for their massive size and speed. Throughout generations, the horse farmers of Evenspark have managed to perfect an animal that can run miles without tiring and outlive the average lifespan of any ordinary horse."

Valen took a step toward her. "But there's more to it. It takes an exceptional rider as well."

Her head tilted down and her white hair fell in front of her eyes. "I've worked hard for many years, training day and night."

"I'm sure you have. You ride with such ease and grace."

The girl rounded the fountain, meeting Valen halfway. "It has always been my dream to ride in the Interkingdom Carriers."

"Now it looks as though you've done it. They will take you in right away."

"I certainly hope so." She raised a small hand and placed delicate strands of her hair behind her ear. Valen resisted the urge to stare. He admired her modesty. She was so humble for such an experienced rider and champion, and for such a beauty of a girl.

A question brimmed in his thoughts. "If it means so much to you, then why did you jeopardize the race?"

The girl did not flinch or turn away insulted. Instead, she held his gaze firmly and responded, "I did not want the healers to risk their lives retrieving her. There was not enough time before the oncoming riders. I had to make a decision."

Valen considered her answer. He was highly impressed that she would put the welfare of another in front of her own dreams. Ravencliff's elite did not encourage philanthropy. "Fate has rewarded you. It must be your destiny."

The girl laughed lightly, like he'd told a joke she'd heard all too often. She stepped toward him, making his heart race. "You make your own destiny."

"I only wish that were so." Valen thought of all the heavy expectations of his impending position as the future king of Ravencliff. "For some of us, it is preplanned." He couldn't believe he'd told his innermost fears and personal challenges to this strange young specter of the night.

The girl studied him, as if she could peer through his crumbling facade and see the true shape of his inner being. Her head cocked to the side, her eyes glinting silver. "That's what the rulers want you to think."

With those earth-shattering words, she turned and disappeared into the burning light of the chandeliers.

Valen was blindsided. Coming from her, he almost believed it. Never had he thought he held his own future in his hands. The king dictated his destiny each day of his life, strategically planning his every task from the moment he could talk for optimum results. Royal princes had no say in the matter. How could the rider assume he was so free?

Looking down at his attire, Valen realized he'd shed all of the garments of his station, leaving only his red-and-black tunic and vest. The woman had no idea she spoke to a future king and, as he studied the empty place where she had stood, he realized he had no way of asking her if she meant what she said, even for a prince.

Valen searched the party for the remainder of the night, scanning waves of faces and darting in between mingling clusters of noblewomen all vying for one another's attention. The music swelled in his ears, diluting his concentration and mocking his search with absurdly pleasant jigs. People swirled around him, a mass of frivolous gowns and velvet capes, obscuring his vision of the entire ballroom. The white rider had vanished as magically as she'd appeared. Before Valen was ready, the golden clock chimed twelve times, signaling the end of the Midnight Ball.

Valen left with great disappointment. He had tasted an elusive sparkle of freedom, the idea of choice, only to have it evaporate on the tip of his tongue. He convinced himself their conversation was not a dream or a hallucination caused by the wine. In so many ways, it would have been easier to let it go.

He hoped he would see her again during his next visit. But as the days passed, all expectations of returning to Evenspark were defeated. The Elyndra grew more and more aggressive, and as the next year came around, it brought tragedy with it. The king proclaimed the land far too dangerous for his son, the heir to the throne, to ride out.

Valen pined for days. He feared he would never see her again and buried the memory of that sunny day in a place where he thought it could no longer haunt him, a place so deep it rooted in the core of his heart.

Chapter 9

Heavenly Gift

Star watched as the mist crept in through a crack in the windowsill. Like a steady stream of smoke, it curled around the base of the glass, collecting in a pool of fog on the wooden floor. She ran her finger through the transparent ribbon, momentarily disrupting the flow. She knew if she tried to plug the crack with her finger, the mist would seep around her skin, streaming like water. In her childhood, she'd spent many afternoons trying to clog the mist's passage to no avail.

Her father constantly smoothed plaster on the walls and in the crevices in the floorboards where stray mist could seep in. He used glue, old towels and melted wax from his candle shop. These paltry devices would keep the mist at bay momentarily, but they did not last forever. Just when he fixed one hole, another would form, whether from the elements, the shifting of the wood, or wear throughout the years. Her father fought a battle that could never be entirely won.

Perched on the downside of the steep hill surrounding Evenspark, her parents' home sat at the edge of the grid just before the outskirts. On a still night, while she lay in bed, she could hear the prattle of the mist blowers a mile away. One day, when she bought their new home, she'd also purchase a cottage nearby so she could keep watch over them as they grew older.

"Star, honey, why don't you find a nice book to read? Or there's this tablecloth that needs sewing—"

"No thanks, Mum," Star replied listlessly, more involved in moving the wisps with her fingertips.

"Come now, you can't just sit there forever."

Star looked up as her mother appeared in the doorway. She was older now, her blond hair turning white like Star's. The fingers Star remembered braiding her long locks were now wrinkled and dry with cracked skin. But she was the same in spirit. Putting her wizened hands on her hips, her mother came right to the core of the matter. "It's been two days."

"And no one has come for me." Star pulled a fuzzy piece of lint off their old couch and threw it on the rug. "My job is lost."

"There's no sense in wallowing in the matter." Star's mother spread her hands in the air. "It's their loss. We all know you are the best rider in Evenspark."

"*Was* the best rider."

Her mother frowned in sympathy, her voice growing plaintive. "Even the best can't win against shifting alliances and politics. You've got to find something else to fill your time. Go to the market and see if they need to make any deliveries in town. Maybe Colins needs some bushels of hay."

"We need more money. The pay Colins will give me for my deliveries won't be worth the trip."

"It's not for money, it's for your own good. You're still so young, Star. Your life is full of endless possibilities. You can't whittle your time away with silly regrets."

"The truth is I didn't just lose my job. I lost my dream of buying you a better house. A safer house."

"My dear." Her mother sat beside her on the pillowed couch. "This is our home. It's always been our home."

Star took her mother's hand and squeezed it. "But the mist—"

"The mist is a nuisance, yes, but we can deal with that. As for the Elyndra, the grid has always held."

"But what if they find a way through?"

"It seems to me you are much more likely to be attacked than any one of us." Star's mother smoothed her hair. "You are the one in danger, Star. You don't think we worry about you?"

Star bit her lip and remained quiet. She hadn't mentioned her recent brush with the Elyndra. It would heighten their concerns. Star knew her mother was right and had no adequate answer to give.

"Anyway, even if you bought us some lavish mansion, we wouldn't leave our home. Besides, what would we do with all of those rich noblemen and noblewomen? Could we actually be happy with neighbors like that?"

Star took in the familiar sight of her mother's old apron, her wayward white hair and her kind eyes. She realized they wouldn't be happy in a lofty house in the inner district. Those were her dreams and not their own.

"Come now, you have enough money saved up for awhile, don't you?"

"Yes, I do." Star's gaze wandered to her riding cloak. "In fact, I have quite a payment right here." Digging in her pocket, Star found the golden trinket box and brought it out for her mother to see. "It's not enough to buy a house, but it could ensure financial security for some time."

She clicked open the latch. The ruby pendant caught the light of the burning candles and glinted, spreading crimson shafts around the kitchen.

"My goodness." Her mother's eyes went wide. "That's quite a gift."

"And quite a giver..." Star didn't have to say any more.

"Why sell such a wonderful present?"

"That's just it. I don't know what it is. It could be just a reward, a payment, something he found on his way out, or it could mean much more."

Her mother held the ruby in her hands, dangling it in front of her eyes to study its shape, as if by looking at it she could read into Valen's own heart. "People give gifts for so many reasons. Only time will tell." She put the pendant back in the box then put her hands over Star's hands, closing the lid. "Let's wait and see. In the meantime, keep it safe."

"It's probably nothing. Why would someone giving away rubies ever be interested in a poor girl like me?"

"Dear Star, you were always so beautiful and unique. When you were born, we stared in awe at your silver eyes and white hair. I thought you were a gift from the heavens above. That's why I named you Star."

"I'm not special. I just worked hard, and now all my diligence has come to naught."

"I don't think it has." Her mother's eyes were kind, her grip strong as she held her daughter's small hands. "I still think you'll do great and wonderful things."

Star shrugged, looking away. She loved her mother too much to deny her.

Her mother's face brightened like the sun peeking through the clouds at midday. "But right now, we need to cook dinner. Your father will be home soon. Come and join me when you escape the brooding prison you've made of our old couch."

Her mother patted her knee and went into the kitchen. Left alone, Star opened the box once again and took out the ruby, feeling the weight in the palm of her hand. She impulsively draped the pendant around her neck, fastening the clasp. It felt heavy on her chest, like it didn't fit her, both physically and in station, but Star ignored the incongruity. She hid it underneath her blouse, the ruby falling in between her breasts, near her heart. After a moment of thought, she joined her mother, helping peel the onions for the stew.

And a wonderful dinner it was. Vegetable dumplings, onion stew and a twisted loaf of wheat bread her father bought in town at the bakery. Somehow the conversation she'd had with her mother lifted a weight off of her shoulders, and she could sit back and enjoy the time with both her parents. They reminisced about taking Star to her first riding lesson, the day their family horse birthed Windracer and Star's first tournament ten years ago.

"Remember, they invited you to the castle," her father said, still proud a decade later.

"That's right," her mother chimed in. "It was the Midnight Ball, wasn't it?"

"Yes, I remember." Star crinkled her nose. "I didn't like it at all. In fact, I slipped away before the clock struck twelve."

A distant thought tugged at Star's memory, but she couldn't quite form any tangible conclusion. Something about that night remained a mystery to her.

Her thoughts were interrupted by an insistent knock at the door.

"Who could that be?" her mother asked no one in particular. "I didn't invite anyone."

"I'll go and see." Her father wiped his hands on his napkin and tossed it on the table. Star sat with her mother, waiting as her father answered the door.

"Maybe it's the young man who gave you the necklace..."

Star shook her head. "No, Mum, he lives in Ravencliff."

"Ravencliff!" Her mother's voice rose and Star had to shush her. "You didn't mention he lived so far away."

"I didn't want you to worry."

Thankfully, her father reappeared in the hallway, silencing the conversation. He turned to Star. "It's for you."

For a moment, Star allowed her heart to hope somehow Valen had ridden through the countryside to visit her, although the idea was preposterous. As she walked to the front room, she recognized Zetta immediately in the failing light.

Zetta stood hunched in an old shawl. Her hair stuck out like an unwound cotton ball and her eyes were sunken in her face, dark and shifty pupils framed by purplish circles. She always looked a bit frazzled, but tonight she was utterly frantic. Every wrinkle in her face seemed crumpled up, making her look ten years older than her middle age.

Star stifled the urge to slam the door in her face. "What are you doing here?"

"There's been a problem in the Interkingdom Carriers."

Zetta's weary face played on Star's heartstrings, and Star opened the door wider. "Come inside, Zetta, where there is more light."

"This is a private matter."

"Of course. I'll make sure my parents retire to their room." Star knew a person could hear anyone talk from any room of the small house, but at this point she didn't care about the Interkingdom Carriers and their secrets. Besides, she would inform her parents of any news once Zetta left anyway.

As she ushered Zetta to the front couch, Star signaled to her parents in the dining room to be quiet and closed the door. She sat across from Zetta in her father's rocking chair. Zetta's features darted in and out of the candlelight. "What sort of problem?"

"Tia rode out two days ago, delivering important letters to Ravencliff. Her horse returned today without her."

She needn't have said more. Star knew there was no hope. But Zetta continued, as if the gory details could not escape her mind. "There was blood on its back."

"Was the horse injured?"

"No."

Silence fell between them. All Star could feel was sympathy, not only for Tia, but for Zetta as well. Her superior would have to answer to those above, and her decisions would be questioned.

"What do you want of me?"

"Forgiveness. I cannot say why I did what I did, but I can say you were right."

"And that's it? Just forgiveness?"

Zetta's shoulders tensed. "No. I need you to ride out and deliver a second set of letters. I've already contacted the senders and allowed time for them to rewrite their correspondence, which must be received."

"Why don't you choose another messenger?"

Star had never seen Zetta's eyes shine so brightly with fear. "No one will go out, not after what happened to Tia. They refuse."

"And what if I say no?"

"Then we will lose all contact with Ravencliff. If no one will ride out, the queen will shut down Interkingdom Carriers. All of our jobs will be gone."

Star was skeptical. "Come, Zetta, there must someone who—"

"No." Zetta's eyes held certainty. "Believe me, I've tried. I've even asked people on the street, anyone who can ride a horse."

"Ravencliff must have riders."

Zetta's gaze grazed the floor, avoiding her eye. "Their fastest one quit our Interkingdom Carriers a few years back. Since then, no one has stepped up to take his place. They don't have the same training academies and riding competitions in Ravencliff that we do."

Star bit her lower lip, thinking fast.

"The carrier's parcel is packaged and ready to go. You can ride out immediately."

Star wouldn't do it for Zetta or even for the Interkingdom Carriers. She would do it for Valen, to get a chance to see him again. "I'll leave tomorrow at dusk."

Chapter 10

Trail of Blood

The metalwork of the grid screeched in Star's wake, covering Windracer's rapid hoofbeats. Pent up for two days with nowhere to run, Windracer burst into a wild stampede, propelling them forward like they were demons fleeing the rise of the sun. Star grasped Windracer's bridle, the breeze whipping her cloak behind her.

This time Star rode prepared. She carried a long sword and a torch stick and wore a sentinel helmet. The metal dug into her head and shoulders uncomfortably, and she didn't like the extra weight it put on Windracer's back. The broad visor made peripheral sight difficult. Her breath echoed in her ears, resounding in her helmet as if the entire countryside could hear. However, it was necessary to protect her from the attacks above.

As Star entered the valley of the moors, she flipped up the visor, looking for any sign of what had happened to Tia. The winding trail was as bare as ever, and the mist cloaked everything beyond twenty feet ahead.

Because of the rainstorm that had swept the land, Tia's horse's tracks would be gone. Star studied the countryside for any sign of a struggle amidst the leafless, scrawny trees and marsh weed, but the moors hid its secrets well. Star searched for Tia's remains, wondering if there was anything left.

She was almost halfway to Ravencliff when she rode over a patch of stained dirt. At first, it seemed the dark soil was still damp from the rain, then Star realized with a chilling eeriness in the pit of her stomach that the sand was dry. The rain had only spread the mess, leaking color down around the raised trail to mingle with the marsh water. The sand was not wet, but tainted with blood.

Star turned Windracer around. She had to go back. The desire to know what happened overwhelmed all other concerns.

As she neared the sight of the blood-smeared road, Star slowed Windracer to a canter. She rounded the scene, studying the shape of the stain. Although it had trickled in all directions, the darkest and thickest trail led off of the road into the marsh to her left.

She led Windracer into the bog, her horse's hooves splashing in the water. She hoped the noise wasn't loud enough to alert the Elyndra to her presence. Holding her breath, Star unsheathed her long sword.

The marsh weeds rose around them, brushing Star's legs as she urged Windracer on and searched the murky waters around them. Anything that had fallen in would have sunk by now, becoming part of the sludge. Even if Tia had made it off her horse and hid in the water, she would have been mortally injured, losing a lot of blood. If she fell unconscious, she would have surely drowned.

But still Star looked for her, scanning the mossy cattails for an article of clothing, an arm or the top of Tia's gray-haired head. She tried not to be spooked by the way the grass clung to her legs, as if the marsh reached out to take her in, or the mist flowing along the water's edge, promising to bring those spindly legs with it. It was the thought of Tia's limp body, floating in the bog like a dead jellyfish, that disturbed her most of all.

Looking up for the first time, Star realized she'd searched in the wrong direction. Above her head, in the forsaken arms of a dead oak tree, hung a white letter bag much like her own.

Star gasped, cursing under her breath. Tia had not made it to the water's edge. She'd been carried away, off her horse and into the misty sky. The letter bag likely fell off her shoulder in mid-flight, the leather handle catching in the knotted branches.

Reaching up with her long sword, Star cut the handle of the bag, dislodging it from the scraggly tree. It fell, taking brittle branches with it on its way down, but the front flap stayed secure and the letters remained inside, unscathed. Star caught the pack before it fell into the depths of the bog.

Her gaze darting swiftly around her, Star secured the second bag to her back and urged Windracer back onto the path. Two letter packs would slow her down. With a quick decision, she threw off her metal helmet and a bag of food rations. The letters were more important.

They took off into the mist. Faced with graphic evidence of her fellow carrier's demise, Star's stomach lurched. She had never seen so much blood. Suddenly, Star realized that Tia, as much as she had despised her, was not the true enemy. The case of the Elyndra was far more serious than a string of harsh words or the loss of a job.

In that moment, Star found a purpose much bigger than any other she'd ever strived for, much more important than any letter she'd ever delivered. Star was going to fight for the freedom of all of her countrymen. She was going to find the source of the Elyndra and kill them all.

Angered by their cruel disregard for human life, Star dared them to attack her again. She cursed the sky above with all manner of words, swinging her sword at the mist as if it, too, was a culprit. But none of the beasts descended. The mist held empty wishes for her revenge.

Guards lowered the drawbridge to Ravencliff and Star rode across it. She glanced back over her shoulder but saw nothing. At least she was no longer afraid.

* * * *

Star sat in her room at the Overflow Tavern with the two letter bags on either side. Her first thought was to match each letter with its copy, making sure the Interkingdom Carriers informed every sender of the accident and each writer had a chance to recreate another letter in its place. Tia's letters were soggy from being in the rain for so long, but the writing could still be read. Star could deliver both copies, just in case the sender had left out important correspondence the second time.

Of course, the head collector's files were accurate, and each letter had its copy. She was almost done sorting when she saw an unapproved letter addressed to Fallon Leer.

It stood out from the pile like a red flag rising against stone, the heavy parchment stamped with the iconic seal. Star dug into her bag and found she had a newer version of the same letter. Zetta had smuggled it through the collectors with success twice.

Suddenly, Star realized why Zetta had chosen Tia to ride out in her place. Star had questioned the first smuggled letter. She had given voice to the breach of protocol with zeal. Had Zetta been afraid Star would turn her in?

Burying a sudden rush of anger, Star took up Tia's version of the letter. It dripped on the floor, soaked through from the rain. Star could almost make out the writing inside. She held the parchment to the candlelight. The ink had run in blurry splotches because of the rain. It was too hard to read.

An idea flickered in her thoughts. No one knew she had two sets of letters. She could open any of the letters in the first set and still deliver the pristine, unopened copies tomorrow. She could break the seal, open it and read what was inside, the reason why Zetta trusted Tia over her.

Star paused. She knew it was blatantly against the messengers' code. If she opened a letter addressed to someone else, she would be stripped of her title immediately and thrown in jail. However, this was not a processed letter. In fact, it wasn't even in the books to begin with. What evidence would Zetta have against her?

She considered reading others' private correspondence ethically wrong, but forcing someone to deliver renegade mail was also questionable. Having her station lowered had been the final motivation that broke her loyalty to Zetta. The thought of it still made the skin on her back prickle with anger.

Before she could convince herself otherwise, Star tore open the seal with shaky fingers. Sitting next to the candlelight, she read.

> *System Date 4671*
> *Letter Receiver: Fallon Leer*
> *Official approval for the subject's termination has been allotted. A payment of three thousand pounds in gold will be awarded upon receipt of the news. Confirmation is contingent upon solid evidence. Subject in question: Prince Valen Crawford of Ravencliff.*

The sender signed it with a printed copy of the seal.

Star stared at the parchment for a long time. Horror at the thought of Valen's assassination clenched her heart and her skin prickled in fear. She calmed herself by turning to more logical thoughts. She had to find the perpetrator.

Her mind churned over endless possibilities. It could be Zetta herself, which was highly unlikely. Zetta was probably only a pawn in a larger game. It could be Vespa, exacting revenge on the man who'd ended their lifelong engagement, but that wouldn't explain the first letter to Fallon Leer. It could even have come from the highest power, Evenspark's illustrious queen, finally damning the ruling house of Ravencliff after its king refused to marry her five years ago. Finally, Star speculated, it could be anyone from Bellanina's family, for they gained a throne from Valen's death.

Star knew one thing for sure. Duty or not, this was the first letter she utterly refused to deliver, even if it came from her own kingdom, a kingdom she once thought was honest and just. Not only would it spark a war, but the subject in question was the man who held her heart, whether she wanted him to have it or not.

Pacing her small room, Star's mind sped, each step bringing a new thought along with it. She needed to find a way into the castle to warn Valen, but she didn't know who to trust. Looking back at the pile of letters scattered on the floor, Star grew eager. Not one of them had a royal seal. She had no way through the main gate and she couldn't show the assassination letter to the guards because one of them may be in on the plot. Besides, this could not wait until morning. If Fallon Leer did not get his response by tomorrow, he could suspect foul play and may flee. She wanted to catch him to put a stop to all of this. She had to act now.

Star halted in mid-step, staring at the foot of her bed, where the bunnyfly had slept only days ago. The ridiculous pet was the key. A secret passage led into the private royal chambers, no doubt. All Star had to do was find it.

Chapter 11

Fire Warrior

Star slipped from the Overflow Tavern in the crux of night with an armful of plaited rope, her long sword sheathed at her side and a torch stick tied to her belt. She paused momentarily by the stables to bid farewell to Windracer, for the horse was not needed tonight, nor could she go where Star's journey led. Besides, she did not wish to put Windracer in jeopardy for her own farfetched plans. This was the first mission on which she would be going alone.

As Star tiptoed down the lonely city streets, she felt as though she had left a part of herself behind. Windracer had been a steady companion at her side, acting as an extension of her own body. Without her, Star felt vulnerable but she had to remind herself a horse could not scale walls.

The archers were stationed at every rampart, and two sentinels stood ten yards apart. Not only did they spy flying Elyndra, but they also kept citizens from approaching the walls of the fortress. For obvious reasons, no one but a journeyman was allowed out. They were all prisoners under siege in their own homes.

Star watched from behind a stone tower, her head peeking beyond the curve of the dark rock. The archers had their backs turned toward the countryside, nervously watching the sky on the horizon. As ordered, their bows were loaded and cocked, pointing down into the mist surrounding the walls.

A shout rang out from the bordering parapet.

"What is it?" the archer closest to Star whispered to his comrade.

"Don't know." The second archer peered down the battlements. "I think they see one."

"Not again." The other archer seemed skeptical. "There's no use shootin' at ghosts."

Then another shout came from the same direction, this one stronger and more incredulous. Star could hear the whiz of arrows flying through the sky. The archers engaged fire.

The men stationed in front of her scurried down the battlements to the source of the commotion. It was just the distraction that Star needed in order to get through to the wall. She suspected they wouldn't leave their posts for long. She didn't have much time. If they saw her, they'd pull her right back up. No one was allowed outside the city. The guards did not want to provoke the Elyndra.

Star ran over to the edge of the wall, peering down between the columns of rock. All she could see was endless mist, but it wasn't the thickness of the haze that surprised her, it was the height. The stable boy's story was true—the mist was rising. It flowed only five feet from the top of the wall, nearly thirty feet taller than just three years ago when Star was given a tour of Ravencliff on her first visit. If it continued at that pace, the miasma would overcome the walls in less than a year.

She tied the rope to the foot of a stone gargoyle decorating the guard tower. After tugging on the knot, she looked around her nervously. The archers yelled from down the battlements, still engrossed in their hunt. With a deep breath, Star climbed onto the rim and leaped.

It was a dizzying feeling to have nothing but mist below her. Star hung in suspension with fog on all sides. Bracing her feet against the sleek rock of the fortress wall, she slowly lowered herself, pace by pace.

She could still hear the commotion on the far side of the wall. The archers had fired multiple rounds, but she'd heard no cry of triumph. Star wondered where the Elyndra had gone. She looked over her shoulder, but the mist obscured any sense of movement beyond the walls.

Suddenly she felt a draft of air lift stray strands of her hair. Their quarry hadn't flown away. Star had lured it to the other side.

Goosebumps formed on her arms and shoulders as the all-too-familiar swishing sound came from above. With one hand grasping the rope, Star drew her long sword and prayed.

The Elyndra dove, coming at her with the force of gravity on its side. Star kicked away from the wall just in time to avoid a head-on collision. But she knew it would be back.

Losing her sense of direction, Star flew through the air, suspended precariously on her rope. She clung desperately with all of her strength, and came back around, hitting the wall hard. Her hand smashed up against the rock, causing her to drop her long sword into the misted depths below her feet.

Panic ran through her veins like a fast-acting poison, distorting reason and logic. Her thoughts scattered in a million directions, none of them coming to any sort of valid action. Looking back up to the battlements, Star hoped the archers had returned to their stations. Maybe they could drive it away with their arrows. But one look revealed no one was there and she had climbed down too far to call to them.

This time the Elyndra came from the side. Star heard the *swoosh* of its wings first and saw two wire-like worms cut through the mist. The spindly antennae were attached to a small head and two large, iridescent black spheres that could only be its alien eyes. Then the legs hovered over her and she screamed. Just as it reached for her, Star loosened her grip on the rope, falling several feet. The Elyndra groped thin air.

The rope burned the palms of Star's hands, but she knew she had to hold on. She couldn't tell how steep the drop was to the ground below. She could hear the wings as they circled round. It was coming back.

Shaking, Star untied the torch stick as her other hand clung to the rope. Next, she dug in her pockets for a match. "Come on, come on." Her fingertips fumbled around in the folds of her front coat pocket. Luckily, they touched the tip of the match. Star almost dropped it as she pulled it out. Swearing, she managed to strike it against the rock, hoping with all of her might it would spark flame.

It did. The torch stick blazed into a fiery light just as the Elyndra came at her again.

This time she thrust the newborn flame at its wings. The Elyndra balked, legs flailing. Star reached out and swung, setting its left side on fire. The flames caught and spread on the wings like on a dry sheet of parchment. The beast teetered in the air before plummeting to the ground below, leaving a swirling stream of gray and black smoke.

Star realized she'd been tensing every muscle in her body. After a long moment of shock, she gradually relaxed, trying to convince herself she was all right. Soon curiosity outweighed fear and she wondered if she truly slew the beast. Making sure she had a decent grip on her torch, Star lowered herself with sore hands the remainder of the way until her feet hit the ground. She was relieved to see her longsword resting on the ground. Star snatched the weapon up and went to investigate.

The stench of burnt wing tissue was almost unbearable. Star covered her nose with her arm as she approached the flames licking their way through the mist. Before her lay the greatest scientific find of her century—the only incapacitated Elyndra ever found. The beast flailed, stumbling toward Star. Some of its legs were broken from the fall, hanging at crooked angles. A glimmering powder coated its right wing, sparkling in a lustrous, rainbow-like play of color. A single black disk in the center of the wing acted as a counterfeit eye.

Because of Star, the left wing was a smoldering stump. Star tried to get closer, but the creature's antennas reached out toward her, twitching in jagged motions.

Star stared into the cold vastness of its multifaceted eyes. She tried to see beyond the predator to the soul that lay dying beneath, but all she saw in those great orbs was ignorance and death.

She circled the beast, staying free of the probing antennae until she could reach around to its torso. In a swift motion, she brought the sword down to end its suffering. The sword sliced easily through its soft inner carapace, stabbing it through its back.

"Fire." Star kicked the mass of tangled legs. "You can fight them with fire." The Elyndra weren't mysterious ghosts or otherworldly demigods. They were living, breathing creatures that could die like anything else.

The body was far too big for her to drag. Gazing up at the lookout tower, Star thought she could pinpoint the location from the walls above. Ravencliff would get a specimen. That is, if she managed to get back in at all.

As the exhilaration from the triumph of battle welled inside her, she had to remind herself the beast was but one in perhaps a hundred, even a thousand. Although it felt like she'd conquered the world, it was a small victory at most. She still had to be cautious.

Holding the torch above her head, Star found her way back to the edge of the wall. Before she'd jumped, she had calculated the exact spot where the bunnyfly had been found in relation to the walls of Ravencliff. The southern side was her best bet at finding the breach.

Star walked along the wall, her gaze scanning the black rock for cracks in the facade, crumbling debris or any sign of an opening. To her chagrin, the wall was solid without as much as a chink in the ebony facade.

Once several feet down the incline toward the mountain, Star suspected the bunnyfly had miraculously flown over the fortress barricade. The terrain grew harder to cross and a scraggly patch of briars and shrubs forced her away from the wall. She almost continued onward but changed her mind, deciding a methodical and meticulous approach would yield better results.

Using her sword, Star cut down the overgrowth. Beneath the tangled mass was a fissure four feet tall and five feet wide. Star ran her fingers over the grooved edges on the wall of the passageway. This was not done by wind, rain or imperfections in the rock itself. These gashes were made by a human tool. Star's first thought was a pick axe, but the rock was far too strong to crack by any metal implement she'd seen forged.

She paused, mulling over the serrations in the rock. Whoever made this passage had devices far stronger than she could imagine. Advanced tools meant human intelligence and power. Star had the sinking feeling she was in far over her head.

Cautiously, she ducked inside. The passageway slanted at a steep incline, carved from the mountain. Star climbed with her torch in hand. There was no way she would stumble through the darkness with no light. Her small stature made it easy to traverse winding turns in the passageway. It took only a few minutes to slip through to the end, where moonlight shone between cracks in the ceiling.

Star blew out her torch. She realized she stood under slates of limestone. Reaching her hands above her head, Star moved one of the slates and hefted herself out of the secret passageway, surfacing underneath large ferns.

Pushing the greenery away, she thought she emerged in a jungle from one of the stories her mother read to her at night as a child. Then, as she emerged from the ferns, she recognized her surroundings as none other than the private atrium where she'd delivered the bunnyfly. It must have slipped through a crack in the granite slabs as the princess studied, plunging down the tunnel and onto the moors.

There was a glass door at the far end of the atrium, opposite the side where she had entered with the guard. She knew one way led toward the front of the castle, meaning the opposite direction would take her to the inner chambers, where the royal family would be sound asleep.

Leaving her torch in the tunnel, Star took off toward the inner castle. The glass door was partially opened, and a thin curtain spilled out into the night, floating listlessly in the gentle breeze. Star poked her head in.

A rocking horse with bridled reins gilded in gold guarded the room. Dolls littered the floor, their hair fanning out to carpet the marble in waves of gold and amber. There a small, canopied bed occupied the far wall of the room, draped in pink veils. At the foot of the bed rested a round basket.

Star pushed the glass door open further, quietly taking a step into the room. She sensed movement at the corner of her eye. The basket shook and a familiar face peeked out. To Star's surprise, the bunnyfly stared at her, its wide eyes large as two moons. It cooed softly, a pleasant sound, like it recognized her.

"Shh." Star waved back the bunnyfly. She could see Princess Bellanina wrapped in blankets like a rosebud, sleeping soundly in her bed.

The bunnyfly moved restlessly in the basket, stirring up sparkles as it jumped, front paws dangling on the edge. The basket wobbled, threatening to fall over.

"No," Star whispered. "You stay still." Cursing her situation, she tiptoed closer to the foot of the princess's bed, where she kneeled and comforted the bunnyfly, running her hands over the smooth velvet fur on its back. The animal nestled back down into the basket with a sleepy chirp.

Swiftly, Star glided around the bed toward the door. The princess shifted, but did not wake. Star held her breath as she opened the door to the hallway, praying the metal hinges wouldn't creak. It opened silently, allowing her to slip through.

She closed the door behind her and collapsed against it, finally letting her breath loose. Messengers were not trained for stealth, nor were they trained to scale walls or find secret tunnels. She was way beyond her expertise.

Thankfully, the late hour ensured no one walked the hallways. Star searched door to door, trying to decipher the room belonging to Valen. The princess had her name engraved on the door, but each room that came after hers did not have any identification at all.

Further down the hallway she found a door painted with Valen's name in silver letters. Star stared in indecision. Her plan seemed like an excellent idea until now. She'd scaled the fortress walls, fought a great flying beast, navigated a secret spy tunnel and now she couldn't knock on a door. What was wrong with her? Had she come all this way to hide like a schoolgirl?

She wondered if he slept in there at all. What if someone else occupied his room that night? What if his room had changed? If she knocked, then the substitute would answer, call out the guards and she'd be thrown in the dungeon or on the streets, in the same place she was before all of this.

Star tried the knob and it turned with no protest. Her pulse quickened as she opened the door.

Chapter 12

Trophy Beast

A single triangular window leaked moonlight through fluttering curtains onto a marble floor cut in diamond patterns. Star tiptoed toward the silhouette of a velvet-draped canopied bed, grateful for the stone. The polished floor didn't creak under her steps like the old wooden boards in her parents' house.

When she reached the bed, Star pulled the curtains back enough to peek in. To her surprise, the sheets were empty. Her heart dropped to her feet. He wasn't there. But the sheets were rumpled like someone had recently slept in them. Star touched the pillowcase and felt warmth.

A person, tall and broad enough to be a man, knocked her to the floor. Star struggled to gain an advantage, wrestling with her attacker. She'd been caught off guard and the fall alone knocked the wind out of her lungs. She brought her foot up to kick him but he was too quick. He caught her booted leg and pushed it toward the floor. Soon he had her pinned, resting his body on top of hers. Star resisted, whipping her hair out of her face and into his. When she looked up, she instantly stilled. "Prince Valen…"

Immediately he loosened his grip. "Miss Nightengale." He seemed pleasantly surprised and more than a little amused. "What are you doing sneaking into my bedroom in the middle of the night?"

Once again, Star was at a loss for words. The proximity of his body to hers distracted her, and the situation was now so embarrassing. She blushed. "I…I have a letter you must see."

The prince let her wrists go. "Right now?"

Star wondered what else he had in mind besides reading letters, but reined in her overactive imagination immediately. Although she lay underneath him, she tried to be formal. "Yes, it cannot wait."

Valen shifted his weight, allowing her to sit up. Star reached into her cloak and brought out the letter. "Do you know of a Fallon Leer?"

The prince's face fell into grave lines as his features grew too complicated for Star to interpret. His eyes were dark in the shadows. "I do, yes."

"Here." She handed him the letter with the broken seal.

"But the seal is broken, you must have—"

"My superior had me delivering secret letters to this man. They were not processed, and so I suspected foul play. It was a decision I had to make."

"My letter to Vespa went unprocessed. Did you read that as well?"

Star was insulted by his assertion. "No, I certainly did not."

The prince seemed disappointed and his expression confused her even more.

"But I did see her reaction, and what a reaction it was." She wanted to ask why he called off the engagement, but it wasn't her place, so she said nothing more.

"That, I did expect." He found a candle and set it aflame, bringing flickering light into the room. Holding the letter close to the candlelight, he read silently as Star watched and waited.

"This is serious news indeed," Valen replied after a long moment of reflection. He looked at her with gratitude. "Thank you for bringing this to my attention."

Star could tell the letter weighed heavily on his emotions. She wanted to reach out and comfort him, but could not find an appropriate gesture. "It was nothing."

Valen pocketed the letter. "Once again, you've gone above and beyond the call of duty."

"That's not all."

His eyebrows quirked. "Have you saved our kingdom while you were at it?"

Brightening his spirits made Star immensely pleased. "Not quite. But I do have something that just might help."

* * * *

As Star brought Valen to the parapet, she told him of her struggle with the Elyndra, the breach in the fortress and the spy tunnel. Valen listened, pursing his lips with a wrinkled brow. When he did speak again, it was not what Star expected.

"You should be more careful. Slaying beasts, scaling walls and sneaking into the castle just to deliver a letter to me?"

"It was an important letter. You needed to know."

"But what if something happened to you?"

He sounded like her mother. A rising strain of frustration boiled in her veins. "Now that you have the information, you can capture the traitor and put an end to this."

Indeed, Valen had already sent his most trusted soldiers to retrieve the assassin and guard the hole in the garden where Star had resurfaced. Valen made certain to relay the orders before they left for the tower's edge. Relief already washed over her like a warm bath. Now she knew he would be safe.

Star crossed her arms, wondering why she had to defend her actions to the prince she'd just saved. "I couldn't chance anyone killing you or the assassin escaping. There wasn't enough time and I had to make a decision."

Valen grew quiet, and Star wondered what thoughts crossed his mind. Perhaps he thought her foolish, impulsive or reckless, or a combination of all three. Star couldn't win this battle no matter what she said.

He put a hand on her shoulder, stopping her on the stone steps leading up to the battlements. "Promise me you'll be more careful."

"I can't promise you anything."

Her words seemed to sting his soul. Star watched as his face turned from concern to discomfort. She felt guilty for being so harsh but had no response at her disposal. They walked the remainder of the way in silence.

Star found her rope tied exactly where she'd left it hours before, marking where the beast lay. Fortunately, the archer had failed to notice the rope when he returned to his post. She touched the knot and turned to Valen. "Scaling the wall is the fastest way to retrieve the beast."

Valen looked at her as though she were a wayward child asking to play at midnight. "No, no, no. Why don't we open the drawbridge and drag it in?"

"And risk that more will come in on the mist? Right into the city?"

Valen inhaled quickly then let out his breath. "You have a point."

"Besides, the archers can cover me. I'll climb down, secure the beast and have it up here in a flash."

Valen's shoulders moved as if a snake slithered between them. "I don't like it."

"It's too big to be dragged through the underground tunnel, and someone has to go out there to secure its carapace with rope. If we leave it down there much longer, the other Elyndra might come and carry it away."

"All right. As long as you'll be careful."

Star smirked. "I always am."

Valen shouted for more archers as Star tied a rope around her waist. Once they had ten of the kingdom's best poised with arrows, he lowered Star down the wall with a blazing torch in her hand. The archers held their bows taut, ready to fire should another beast attack.

Once she hit the bottom, Star tied the rope to the Elyndra's body, wrapping it around the circumference of the stomach and back several times before tying a triple knot. The strangeness of her proximity to the killer that almost stole her life hours before tickled the hairs on her neck. A few times she swore it moved out of the corner of her vision and threw herself back on her rump just to stare into its dead eyes once again.

"All set." Star tugged on the rope. "Now, heave!"

She could hear the hefty grunts of several of Ravencliff's largest soldiers as the rope tightened and they dragged the creature toward the wall. She made sure the knot was secured and the entire body hauled. As the creature's body hit the wall, Star jumped onto its back, her cape swirling behind her. The men pulled her and the Elyndra up in a series of groans and heaves.

The men's faces stared in shock as she rose above the rim of the fortress. Of course, the Elyndra captured most of the attention, but she was the heroine who brought it down.

Once over the wall, Star helped them pull the carcass over the ledge. It fell onto the battlements with a thud and a stink that must have wafted all the way back to the castle itself.

Valen told the soldiers to keep their distance as the alchemists slowly approached the dead Elyndra, their experimental tools in hand. As they took specimens to study, Star watched as the Elyndra's wing changed from sparkling iridescence to powdery dust.

"Look." She brushed her finger over the powdery wing. The sparkles fell from it to reveal a thin layer of filmy skin. Glitter coated her fingertip.

"Seems like they can't survive out of the mist." A senior alchemist peered through thin spectacles at Star's finger. "They dry out like fish out of water."

"Then if we somehow can get rid of the mist…"

"We can be rid of them," Valen finished for her. Along with the alchemist, Star had just provided the answer to everyone's largest problem.

Star looked to the horizon. "The mist, it flows south."

"Yes." Valen leaned over the wall's edge. "It comes from the north."

"Why? What produces it?"

Valen squinted as he looked into the unknown. "Weather conditions, perhaps. I'm not sure."

A sudden urge to act pounded in her forehead. She felt as though they all stared at their own deaths but did nothing about it. "Someone is going to have to find out. Look." She leaned her arm over the edge. "The mist is much higher than it's been in the past. It's rising."

Valen frowned. "I know. It's been happening for the last ten years."

"Then why don't you do something about it?"

"What?" Valen put his arms out in frustration. "You tell me, what should we do? We've been building the wall higher now for decades."

"You can't just keep building higher. That's just denying there is a problem. You need to nip it right at the source."

"What should we do, Miss Nightengale? Pray for nicer weather?"

Another voice shot through the crowd. "Or build a bunch of ramshackle mist blowers and cage ourselves like frightened animals?"

Star whirled around. She recognized the smoothness of the voice, edged with the deadpan drawl of the outskirts.

Fallon Leer stood before them, a soldier on each arm. Surprisingly he looked complacent, standing straight with his head tilted upward like he owned the world. His eyes flickered under heavy lids, revealing nothing. Star noticed this time he wore a shirt, the black material covering his tattoos.

"That's enough." The prince tightened his fists. Star noticed he defended her.

"We've captured him, Your Highness." The soldier on Leer's right arm tightened his grip. "He was in his house in the outskirts. He appeared to be waiting for someone or something to arrive."

Leer spoke of his own accord, his accent jovial and light. "So, Prince Valen, we meet again."

But Valen was not in a mood for conversation. He looked to the guards, ignoring Leer's devilish greeting. "Take him in for questioning. I'll join you in a few moments."

Star's mind ticked away. So they had met before, Valen and Leer. She wondered how they knew each other.

Leer looked back over his shoulder, and his next words to Valen gave her even more questions to ponder. "What's wrong? You don't want to reminisce about old times?"

Star watched as Valen's gaze followed Leer as he strutted away, guards in tow. She couldn't imagine what it would be like to face the rogue ordered to kill her and then have him mock her in front of her own guards. Personally, she would have spat foul words in his face right then and there, but Valen stood silent. Star wished she had the same poise and reservation. Perhaps if she did, the instance with Zetta would have turned out much smoother. She admired Valen for his diplomacy. The more time she spent at his side, the more drawn she was to him and his subtle ways.

Star reined in her swooning notions by grappling with the situation at hand. At least she'd solved one problem. But something about the direction of the mist tugged at her thoughts, bringing the Elyndra back into question in her mind. Suddenly, it all came together like a drawing that changed meaning when looked at in a different way. The answer was right in front of her. "That's it. I know now what to do."

"What are you talking about?" Valen returned his attention to her, his eyes foggy with distant thoughts.

"Someone needs to follow the mist to its source, to find out where it comes from and why. Perhaps it will also bring us to the Elyndra's lair."

"And who's going to do that?" It seemed to Star that, by the sarcasm in his voice, Valen already knew her answer. But she declared it aloud anyway.

"I am."

Chapter 13

Riding Partner

"Miss Nightengale." Valen stressed her name as they descended the narrow, twirling steps tumbling down to the dungeons. "I'm sure you are aware every journeyman braving beyond the protection of these walls has never returned."

"I'm not a journeyman. The journeymen looked for other civilizations and lands to colonize. My mission is different. I'm looking for answers."

"It seems to me what you seek is more intangible than anything anyone has ever looked for." Valen paused on the steps, taking her by the arm. "Have you considered there aren't any answers out there? That life is just the way it is?"

Star wanted to speak but couldn't think of anything to say. The truth was she hadn't thought about that. She pulled away from his grasp and resumed her descent. "It's hard to fail, but it's worse to have never tried," she called over her shoulder.

The stairway grew darker and Star felt thankful that torches were lit in sconces on the stone walls. Flimsy strands of web draped the walls, wafting up on the breeze she created as she led the way into the bowels of Ravencliff. The floor was dank with grimy sludge, making the footing slippery. Although she didn't want to touch the thin metal railing, she found it was necessary to hold on to steady her slick steps.

Star could tell from the dual guards posted outside the rotting wood door that Leer's cell sat at the bottom of the staircase, third on the right. As she approached, she noticed a small, iron-barred window at the top of the door's arc. Ignoring the men at watch, Star stood on the tips of her toes and peered through. She could see Leer in the corner, sprawled out on a bench, one leg dangling above the floor and the other bent as though he lounged in a tavern. Guards had shackled both his wrists to chains coming from the wall. Eyes closed, he appeared to be resting, seemingly undisturbed by his predicament.

Star turned back to Valen as he caught up to her. "Are you sure you want me in there for the questioning?" Second thoughts about the whole encounter flew through her mind. It was not wise to get involved in Ravencliff's intricate justice system. However, looking at Valen and the way his eyes beseeched her, she knew she had already enlisted when she'd brought him the letter. In fact, she had committed herself a long time ago, the day her eyes caught sight of Valen in the halls of the inner sanctuary and her heart claimed him as her own.

"Yes, please. I need a witness. You saw the letters exchanging hands. If it's not too much trouble…"

Star sighed. "All right."

Valen nodded and the guards opened the thick wooden door with a skeleton key and heaved. The door swung out from the woodwork reluctantly, rusted hinges creaking.

Leer sat up slowly, stretching his tattooed muscles, and smirked. "Greetings, Prince Valen, Miss Moon Hair. Come for a visit? I must say your accommodations are," he looked around in a sweep of the cell, "less than satisfactory."

"Leer, I'm not in a mood for your antics right now," Valen said with authority. "Your life is in serious danger…again."

"Has the messenger told on me then?" Leer sent Star a stray smile. Unable to meet his sparkling dark eyes and roguish grin, Star looked away.

Valen took a step forward, placing himself between Star and Leer. "I have a letter here from Evenspark, addressed to you, concerning my assassination."

"Yes, well, I knew that was coming," Leer replied casually. "Has it occurred to you, cousin, that I was going to intercept it? That I was playing along the whole time?"

Cousin? Star's thoughts leaped. Fallon Leer and Prince Valen were related? Instantly she saw the resemblance in their faces. The bridge of the nose and the set of the eyes were identical, though Valen's features were more refined and noble, while Leer's were rugged and broader. Both men were strikingly handsome in their own way. Valen had a subtle inner strength while Leer's appeal exuded outward power and inner mystery. Star found herself gawking and had to pull her eyes away to concentrate on the conversation at hand.

"That is your stance, then?" Valen asked him.

Leer raised his hand, palm up, as if to say he could offer nothing more.

Valen looked to Star. "Was there any indication of this either way?"

Star had to remind herself what he referred to. That Leer intercepted the letter to protect Valen? How would she know? She was just the messenger. "No, no indication either way."

"And this is the man who accepted the first letter?"

"Yes. This is him. He expected it."

Valen seemed to be considering many issues at once. Star could sense his inner turmoil. She suspected he yearned to believe his cousin. She studied Leer's timeworn features and tried to find any indication of his purpose, but she could not penetrate his tough facade. All she saw was a man hardened by a rough life, confronting a privileged cousin who had the kingdom in his hands. The situation did not bode well.

"I must think on this. My guards will question you further." Valen turned to leave. "Come, Miss Nightengale, we need to report his position to the authorities."

Valen led Star out of the cell. As the guards closed the door behind them, she fought the urge to look back. She did not want to give Leer another reason to tease her. Valen gestured to the winding stairwell and they began the ascent back into light. Dawn would break soon and the morning sun would peek over the horizon. Star was eager to see it, for the dark of night had settled in her eyes and she felt it would never go away.

"I didn't know he is your cousin." Star studied Valen's back as if she could look into the inner workings of his heart.

"Not many people do." He paused on the stairway. "We were friends once, back when we were small boys. Our mothers were sisters and when they went out together, they brought us along. We went riding, played cards and chess, all the typical family activities. A friendly competition developed between us, but it became clearer the older we grew I was to be king and the rivalry turned sour. I think the inequality of the situation weighed heavily on him. I promised him that, as king, I would see to it that he would have everything I had, but that didn't seem to placate him. He wanted power, prestige and wealth, and he wanted to gain it for himself, not be given the scraps from his younger cousin."

Valen rubbed his face with his hand, as if to wipe away his memories. He gestured for her to keep climbing. "The first major rift between us happened the day my mother died."

Star had heard an accident claimed his mother's life, but no one knew exactly what transpired that day. The royal family refused to speak of it. She was surprised he confided in her, a messenger from another kingdom without an ounce of royal blood running through her veins. It meant he trusted her.

"I remember it clearly, like the instance froze in my mind, a timeless picture."

Suddenly Valen's footsteps were silent. He froze in mid-step, clinging to the railing like it held his salvation. His eyes grew distant, looking beyond the stone to the ground outside the fortress walls. She walked back to him, stopping one stair above so her head was even with his own. "Go on."

"We were fishing out by Ellis Lake. This was back almost ten years ago, when the Elyndra were held at bay by archers and groups strolled the countryside with a guarded retinue."

Valen clutched the railing, the back of his hand turning white. "My mother and Fallon's mother were beading pearl necklaces on the shore. They called to us to come in for the day. Darkness came and the mist thickened around the water's edge. I wanted to go back immediately, but Fallon insisted we linger. Ambitious and insatiable as always, he wanted to try for one more fish."

Anxiety bubbled in her stomach as she listened, as if the rippling waters lapped at her feet while she watched the mist flow in an ominous tide. Part of her wanted him to stop right there, but a larger part needed to know his pain. "Go on." Star placed a hand on his shoulder. "It's all right, I'm listening."

Valen nodded, looking down at the moss-crusted floor. "We fought. I finally convinced him to help me paddle back to shore. By the time we reached the shoreline, the mist seeped all around us, pouring in like water over a cliff. Our surroundings changed from peaceful to precarious in moments.

"We had stayed out too late, but Fallon's anger overshadowed his fear. I'd caught more fish and he couldn't deal with defeat. When I held up my catch of fish to my mother, he ran off into the mist. His mother boarded the carriage to take us back to Ravencliff and was unaware, but my mother had stayed to see we reached the shore safely.

"I remember the beads falling on the beach around my feet like scattered hopes. At first I thought I'd tipped a basket over. When I turned around, I saw my mother had dropped the baskets of necklaces to run after him. I watched as the trail of her indigo shawl vanished into the mist. The archers were already in pursuit. I struggled to run after them, but my guards locked me down. They could not chance losing their future king."

Valen let out a long sad breath. "Fallon was the only one who made it back."

Star covered her mouth with her hand. "My goodness, Prince Valen, I'm so sorry."

He waved her concerns away. "I'm not telling you this for your pity. And it's not meant to upset you either."

Sniffing back the tears that were already brimming in her gray eyes, she wiped her face with her sleeve. "I'm okay. Please, keep talking. I want to hear the whole story."

Pearls of sweat sprinkled his forehead and Valen wiped them away. "If you wish." But he didn't continue. They stood there on the uneven steps with awkward silence falling between them.

"That doesn't explain why he lives in the slums," Star said, wrinkling her brow, "when he's related to the future king."

His gaze returned to Star as if he were pulled away from a stray thought. "Yes, I'll get to that. I tried not to blame him for my mother's disappearance. As we grew older and assumed our separate lives, I endeavored to trust him, to strengthen the blood bond between us, but he fought it. He didn't want my friendship or my peace offerings, and he didn't need them either. All on his own, he became Ravencliff's greatest messenger to ever live. He moved to Evenspark to join up with the Interkingdom Carriers. He rode with them for many years, perhaps quitting just before you won your post."

Star thought back to all of the riders she'd met during the years. "I have no recollection of him." Surprisingly, the thought of missing his presence in the Interkingdom Carriers made her sad, like she'd missed a great opportunity to meet a legend before he fell to tragedy.

"It doesn't matter." Valen's tone sounded bitter, as if he tried to be proud of Leer's accomplishments but his hard feelings got in the way. A heavy weight burdened her heart in a deep melancholy at the estrangement of two cousins. She wished she could bring them back together and heal their relationship.

"So that's why he has the horse tattoos?"

Valen blinked. "You've seen his tattoos?"

Star blushed. "He was half naked when I knocked on his door."

"Figures." Valen rolled his eyes. "He never liked to dress in formal attire."

Whether it was Leer's reluctance to dress up or Valen's distaste of half-naked men, Star found his comment amusing. She stifled a smile and forced herself to think about the matters at hand. "That's why he knew Zetta."

"Who's Zetta?"

"The superior of Evenspark's Interkingdom Carriers. She knew who to send the letter to because he'd been a messenger previously."

"Interesting." Valen's eyes shifted as if his mind were hard at work, calculating. "The treachery lies so deep within the system, and so high up."

Star pursed her lips. "It could be anybody over there."

"Hmm." This time Valen put a hand on her shoulder. "We'll get to the bottom of it. We aren't done with our questioning."

"He won't tell you anything, even if he does know."

"It depends if he wants his reputation cleared. We shall see."

Valen began ascending the steps once again but Star did not follow. "You didn't tell me why he was thrown out of the Royal Guard in the first place."

"He wasn't. He quit a few years back."

"What?" Star couldn't believe the twist in conversation. Valen skipped several paces ahead and she had to take two steps at a time to catch up. "What for?"

Valen shrugged. "I don't know. He just up and quit one day. His horse is still in the stables here at the castle. The poor beast waits for another journey that will never come." His attention strayed toward Star and he smiled, his eyes wistful. "Anyway, why don't I see to it my page delivers your letters? You've been up all night and need to rest."

"Yes, I have a long journey to prepare for."

"Back to Evenspark, I presume."

Although he said it, Star knew Valen's hope was empty. Her tone grew sly. "If only it was that easy."

"Come now, you can't go saving the world all by yourself."

"Who's going to volunteer to go with me?" Star knew she had him in a bind, his duty sitting between both of them like a wall of bricks, but part of her wished he would choose her over his station.

"You know I would go if I could."

Star kept her face stoic, not showing any inclination either way. "You're the great ruler in training. They would never let you."

"I know. And it would be irresponsible of me to run away."

"It's a death sentence for anyone else. No one can ride as fast as I can. They would be left behind."

With her words, Valen suddenly froze.

"What? What did I say?" She thought back to her last statement. Then suddenly the answer dawned on Star. Leer.

"No." Valen grabbed her arm. "You're not going with Fallon."

Star shook off his grip and walked back down the steps. "It just might be the one thing that can redeem him and the one way we will find anything out."

"Did you hear anything that I've said about him? He can't be trusted." Valen followed Star to the dungeons. "He's shifty, and he's always looking out for his own good. He'd leave you stranded if it suited him best."

"Look, Prince Valen." Star turned around to face him. "I can take care of myself."

"All I'm saying is that you'll have enough to worry about out there. You don't need an extra liability."

"Would you prefer I go alone then?"

"I'd prefer you didn't go at all, but seeing as I can't forbid you, and you're the best rider there is and the kingdom is on the verge of disaster, well, then…" Valen threw his arms up in the air. "Go ahead, ask him. He's all yours."

Star was so overcome with Valen's consent she threw her arms around him, flinging him off balance on the steps. They teetered backward together and then settled in each other's arms. She spoke with her eyes closed, holding him close. "Thank you for believing in me."

Valen whispered in her ear, "I've always believed in you."

Star pulled away, confused. "Always? But you've only known me for a few days."

"There is something I must confess." Valen leaned his head in to gaze into her eyes. "I didn't know it at first, it was only a vague sense I've seen you before. But it came to me one night in a rush of memory."

Star waited patiently. Ever since that day in the crowded hallways of the inner sanctuary, she'd wondered why he looked at her so strangely, but never found the courage or tenacity to ask.

"I attended your first riding tournament. I sat as a spectator in the bleachers. I watched you go back to save the woman who'd fallen off her horse, and then overtake the entire race and win with no contest."

Star nodded. "That was me, yes." Another memory tugged at her senses, something about the Midnight Ball after the closing ceremonies, but try as she might, she could not resurrect it.

"I believed in you then, and I believe in you now."

They stood that way for some time, not knowing what to do next. Although she'd pulled back, he still held her in his arms. She wanted him to be the one by her side during her journey. She almost mouthed the words to ask, but her sense of honor held her back.

When he did speak, his voice broke on the words. "Come now, let's find you a riding partner, shall we?"

* * * *

Leer lounged exactly where they'd left him on the bench, sprawled out on his broad back and whistling at the ceiling boards. "Missed me already?" he sang out as Valen and Star entered the cell.

Valen crossed his arms. "We have an offer."

Leer cracked his knuckles and sat up, tilting his head as if to work out a chink. "Let's hear it then."

Valen's nod in her direction reassured Star. He was going to let her lead. "I'm traveling north to investigate the source of the mist and find the lair of the Elyndra. I'm the fastest rider in Evenspark and need an equally fast companion to accompany me."

Star saw surprise flicker on Leer's face. She didn't know if it was the madness of the offer or the fact he'd underestimated her.

"Protect her, bring her home safe, and you are free." Valen held out his palm as if he offered the world.

Leer laughed softly. "A fool's errand. You'll be lucky if either of us come back alive."

Valen was unsympathetic. "It is what it is, and let me remind you that treason against your government is punishable by death."

"And an easier death it would be." Leer's brows rose. "A mere rope burn compared to being eaten alive."

Valen turned around, his face crinkling in disgust. "Come, Miss Nightengale, he's not interested."

Star opened her mouth to press further, but the look in Valen's eyes told her she'd be wasting her breath. She followed him toward the door of the cell.

Leer stood, his shackles clinking. "Wait."

Valen rested his arm against the cell door and closed his eyes, but Star turned around and met Leer's gaze.

Leer skimmed over her and looked at Valen's back. "All of my grievances would be pardoned?"

Valen sighed but did not turn around. "If she's brought home safely, then yes."

Star thought the prince's rewards were a bit much. Valen placed everything on the table for her quest. Although his extravagance made her angry, her heart swelled with wonder. He actually did believe in her.

Leer smiled at Star like she'd just granted him his every wish. "Done."

Chapter 14

Journeyman's Voyage

Saying farewell was harder than Star thought. Two days had withered away since the conversation in Leer's cell, and she was no more ready to leave Valen now than she had been in the dungeon, but every day she waited placed the fortress in higher jeopardy. The mist rose and the walls surrounding Ravencliff stood like a weak dam ready to crack under nature's onslaught. Star wondered how the mist blowers coped with the worsening conditions back at her home in Evenspark. She hoped her parents were safe.

Since no journeymen had ever come back, there were no maps or charts of the territory in the north, only crude projections assumed by Ravencliff's best geographers and cartographers. She planned to ride in the direction of the oncoming mist. Valen supported her plan, although he expressed his worries at her safety, and any path that got Leer out of his cell seemed agreeable.

Star stuffed her pockets full of matches. There were tinderboxes tucked into her belt, breeches, tunic and saddlebag. She was not going to take any chances that a pack might get waterlogged or fail to ignite. She also had a bundle of torch sticks tied to Windracer's saddle, the best blazing torches in the land provided by the prince's alchemists.

She thought it was wise to begin the journey when the first light filtered through the clouds to make the most of the day before darkness fell. Twilight hung in the air, heightening the suspense and anticipation fizzling in her veins. Soon morning would shine on the horizon, bringing with it a blazing sun. Star looked into the sky with weary eyes. In moments, the golden sphere's rays would not be able to reach her. In a few nervous heartbeats, she'd be unreachable by everyone in Ravencliff.

At least she was not going alone. Star chanced a look over at Leer. He was saddling his horse, Wildfire, intently inspecting each fastening and every knot in the reins. She handed him an extra torch stick. "You're sure she's ready for a journey after lounging in the stables for so long?"

Leer quirked an eyebrow. "I just rode her last night and she's got enough bundled energy to fly. Heck, she'll give Windracer a run for it."

Star resisted the urge to scoff at him. She didn't like the thought of someone riding as fast as she could, especially after years of him dallying. "We'll see about that."

Leer took a step toward her and bowed his head so that his lips brushed her hair. His voice was barely a whisper. "I'd be more concerned about Valen's safety. He looks as though he's got the plague."

Ignoring Leer's proximity, Star watched Valen as he talked to the drawbridge guards. His expression turned grim and complex. Star could tell he was nervous by his shifting glances, his face ever changing as the weather on a windy day. She wanted to reassure him everything was going to be all right, but she felt awkward comforting him in front of Leer, and she wasn't sure everything *was* going to be all right. It would be a false guarantee, an empty promise.

Valen ended his conversation with the guards and ran toward them. Leer spoke, his voice bringing her back from her wistful thoughts. "Gear is set." He patted Wildfire on the hind leg. "We shouldn't tarry much longer."

"All right then," Star agreed and looked to the guard. "Open the gate." She took a step to mount Windracer, but Valen grabbed her arm and held her back.

"You don't have to do this." His eyes were sad, framed in dark circles from sleepless nights. They hadn't talked much since the incident in the stairwell, partly because Star avoided his concerns and partly because she saw something blossoming between them, felt something that she'd never experienced before. It was frightening how much she wanted him despite the fact that it would ruin both kingdoms. She almost convinced herself he felt the same. She pushed the thought aside. It was better off this way.

Star pulled her arm away and mounted Windracer. "What else am I going to do? Where else am I going to go? My job is corrupt, my superior is the enemy. Who can I trust? To go back to Evenspark now would be far more dangerous than dealing with the Elyndra."

As if to prove her point, the wheels of the drawbridge turned. The rumble of the gate had begun.

Valen took a step toward her. "You could stay here."

Star looked at the lowering drawbridge, failing to meet his eyes. "My life was back in Evenspark. What could possibly be left here for me?"

She clamped her mouth like she'd said too much all at once. Valen took a breath to speak but held his words back as if a sudden thought gripped him. Instead, he offered her meager words. "Be careful."

Star pulled a stray wisp of hair back over her ear. "I always am."

The drawbridge hit the ground with a muffled thump. Leer sat on Wildfire, pacing before the gate like a leopard in a cage. He shouted over his shoulder, "Come on, Miss Adventure. You don't want to miss your appointment."

Star rolled her eyes at Leer before looking back to Valen once more. "I will get to the bottom of this. If there's a way to halt the mist and stop the Elyndra, I will find it." She gestured to Leer with a flick of her eyes and her voice fell to a whisper. "I'll also find out who is behind those plans. If Leer knows anything, I'll get it out of him."

"Just return home safely." Valen stepped back to allow Windracer room to gallop. His cloak fluttered in the breeze around his ankles, shifty like his own varying affections.

Leer yelled out a cry, spurring Wildfire into action. Star snapped her reins and Windracer took off seconds later. It was too late when Star realized she'd left yet again without saying good-bye.

* * * *

Riding with Leer was like dancing with a partner who whisked her off her feet. Star had never experienced anything like it before. Windracer and Wildfire encouraged each other, weaving in and out of one another's paths, racing head to head. She found it exhilarating and, if the countryside wasn't so dangerous, it would have been great fun.

"Come now, you can't go any faster?" Leer called over the din of hoofbeats and wind roaring in her ears.

"I was going easy on you!" Star spurred Windracer forward with a kick of her heels. She realized she had underestimated Leer. Although he weighed more than her, Wildfire stood an inch higher than Windracer, able to carry the load as easily as Windracer supported her weight. It was a magnificent sight to watch the horse's muscles heave in synchronicity with Leer's rising and falling muscular figure.

It was only when the earth grew jagged they were both forced to slow down. Unlike her runs between kingdoms, this time there was no beaten-down path. They were going where few had gone before and from where no one had ever come back.

Unlike the marshes in the south, the north sprawled out into moorland, sprinkled with tufts of dry grass and slabs of granite jutting out in spiky protrusions like the ridged backs of dragons. Although the terrain was lonesome, Star had the distinct feeling they were being watched. Each step brought them closer to the Elyndra's turf, making them trespassers in a hostile land. The mist grew thick as old molasses, clinging to everything it touched. Star could feel the coolness of the wisps on her face and the moisture dampening her hair.

They rode throughout the day and into the darkening twilight, staying close to Ravencliff's mountains as if they were the lifeline to their countrymen and their home. Star hoped they could find shelter within the crooks of the crags.

Leer roamed the perimeter of the mountains, searching for any crevice where they could take refuge from the oncoming night as Star watched the sky with a blazing torch in hand. She brandished the flames, challenging the darkening sky and searching the mist for any sign of life, but there was only emptiness around her.

"It's all right, girl, he'll be back soon." She ran her fingers through the tangles in her horse's mane. Her voice sounded weak against the backdrop of thickening mist and shadows.

When hours had passed and Leer had not come back, worries crept into Star's thoughts. The evening had given into night and the darkness pressed in on her. She thought she heard whispers on the wind, guttural utterances speaking an archaic language she did not recognize or, perhaps, her imagination conjured up.

Star swung her torch in wild arcs but could see nothing beyond the mist. She tried to remember how she got there in the first place and Leer's face as he explained he'd return as soon as he found shelter. A clinging doubt deepened in her mind. She felt as though she had stumbled into the afterlife and was trapped in the place between the living and the dead. The desolate countryside was made for devilish nightmares. Had she truly made it this far? What if she'd fallen and hit her head, only to be picked off the earth by an Elyndra? What if she joined the dead?

She was relieved beyond words when Leer's torch became a growing glow in the distance, followed by the sound of Wildfire's hoofbeats. The comfort of a familiar image brought her back to the tick of time itself. After collecting her rambling thoughts, she mounted Windracer and met him halfway. Star covered her diminished composure with an accusation. "You were gone for so long."

Leer shifted his weight in the saddle. In the firelight, Star could see the weariness in his features. Perhaps he had not had the easiest time alone either.

She let her indictment drop with a sigh. "What did you find?"

"There is a cave several hundred feet from here. If we build a fire by the entrance, we should be safe for tonight."

Eager to get out of the maddening mist, she stared at Leer like he'd given her salvation. "Wonderful. Let's go then."

But Leer was not so enthusiastic. His eyes were dark and guarded. "You will not be so cheerful once you see what is inside."

"Is it dangerous?" Star pictured a cavern with Elyndra hanging from the ceiling like bats.

Leer shook his head. "Not at all."

"Then what's the problem?" Star had to work to suppress her frustration.

"Let's just say that we weren't the first to find the hiding spot."

His words haunted Star all the way to the cavern. She wanted so badly to inquire further but respected his silence. If he had trouble speaking of it, then it would be easier for her to wait than cause him more discomfort, even if he was a rogue. Besides, she found it hard to talk to him. Silence fit him best. To pull words out of him would be to make a one-legged man dance.

Leer had found the cavern out of sheer luck. Hidden behind an outcrop of tangled weeds, the entrance was but a slit in the mountain's edifice.

"How did you ever find this?" Star dismounted, immediately thinking of the secret tunnel outside the fortress. Maybe she'd found the spy.

"I followed his marks, scratches in the rock wall."

"Whose marks?"

Star walked inside and Leer moved to stop her. "Star, wait."

"I'm tired of speaking in half sentences. If you won't tell me what's in there, then I'll have to go and see for—"

Star froze in her tracks and screamed. Hunched against the side of the cavern wall was a skeleton, clothed in tattered travel gear, its bony fingers holding the remnants of a leather-bound journal.

Although she'd seen a great flying beast, a pool of blood and an assassination letter all in the course of a few days, Star was unprepared for her first look upon the dead. She stood above the corpse, covering her mouth in both hands, her eyes wide. It took long moments for her to regain control of her emotions.

"What? You've never seen a dead man before?" Leer appeared to be amused.

"You didn't tell me that he was in here." Star hugged her shoulders, trying to get hold of herself.

"I said you wouldn't like it." Although Leer wasn't offering an apology, she could see a glint of guilt in his eyes. Maybe now he'd have more to say instead of keeping every word to himself.

"Well, I'm not sleeping in this cave with this corpse." Star pushed by him to the entrance of the cave and looked away. "You're going to have to move him."

Leer shrugged off her remark. Instead he pulled the journal from the body and held it out for her to see. "Look, he was a journeyman. It's written in their distinctive shorthand."

"I can see that." Star's emotions waged inside her body, the curiosity fighting against her queasy stomach. She had learned their script when she studied to be a carrier in Evenspark. Zetta insisted every carrier study the journeyman's handwriting in case anyone ever received a letter from one of them. Star had always thought of it as irrelevant and frivolous busywork. The journeymen's language had died out since none of its writers ever came back. Tonight she was glad she'd paid attention. She took the dusty book in her hands.

"He probably got stuck in here." Leer looked out of the staggered opening. "Unable to leave and find food or water."

"I wouldn't put it above the Elyndra to have trapped and kept him here in an eternal siege." Star flipped through the pages. Each journal entry was dated approximately one hundred years back, ending at the turn of the last century.

Leer led the horses in, securing them to an outcropping in the wall. "Well? What does it say?"

"Not much. Just weather recordings and charts south of here."

"Does it say what happened to him?"

"I'm getting to that part." Star turned to the last entry. She was silent for a long time, reading. Leer approached behind her, glancing over her shoulder. She blinked and squinted. "I think he went crazy. He talks of strange sightings, people scurrying around in brown robes."

"People? Out here? Are you sure you're reading that right?"

"Yes." Star rolled her eyes. "I'm reading it correctly. He says he sees them in the night, talking to the beasts and pressing boxes with buttons on them."

"He did go crazy." Leer ran a hand through his dark hair. "Let's hope we don't start to see them too."

Chapter 15

Spy

Valen stopped before the massive oak door and hesitated as if he were about to throw himself into battle. He adjusted his ceremonial baldric, released a deep breath and secured his thoughts before they raced out of control. He had to remind himself it was only a meeting and his father was only a man who buried his grief and problems under flamboyant distractions and trivial pursuits.

His knock was steady and certain. He could hear his father's weary voice from the opposite end of the room. "Come in."

The prince did as ordered. He opened the door and saw his father lounging on the throne, surrounded by empty wine glasses and platters of half-eaten food. A servant scurried away, bowing ceremoniously before passing Valen on his way in.

"Ah, my dear son."

Whenever Valen stood before the king, he saw a mixture of pleasure, pride and sadness wash over his father's wrinkled features. Valen was his first born, his only son. He was also a constant reminder of the wife he'd lost. Valen did not have the broad brow and chubby cheeks of his father. Instead, he had his mother's vibrant eyes, her upturned nose and her high cheekbones. He could not disguise his father's memories.

"Father, I must speak with you concerning Fallon."

The king sat up slowly, crumbs falling onto the floor from his stomach, and beckoned him closer with a wave of his hand. "Yes, so I've heard from the royal officers. Tell me, why did you let him go? You know the punishment for such a crime."

"Because I'd rather shed my own blood than that of a family member, however incriminated. There's been enough death these days."

The king shrugged. "I suppose sending him out on that lunatic quest was punishment enough, heh?"

Valen held back an urge to wince. "Father..."

"What's done is done. Whatever you want to do, my boy, I'll support you."

Although the confidence his father had in him was reassuring, Valen wished his father cared more about the happenings in Ravencliff. Instead, the man whiled away his time with his young wife and games of cards. Valen practically ruled as a surrogate king already.

"Now, tell me about what happened with Vespa. I hear you've cut off the engagement."

This was precisely why Valen did not want to consult his father about anything. "I know that our dealings with Evenspark have been tumultuous at best. But I don't think my life should have any bearing on that."

His father sighed. "Alas, my son, you know it does. Have you forgotten our history? The sundering of our people in two different societies when the mist first appeared ages ago?"

Valen bit back a retort. He'd heard the history so many times, but he let his father continue out of respect.

His father recited the memorized scriptures. "The people of Evenspark built a cage and imprisoned themselves like cows in a butcher shop, using ramshackle devices to blow back the mist. We, the proud and free people of Ravencliff, decided to build into the mountain, to construct high walls to hold the mist back. We have no cage over our heads, and we do not live in fear. As the only prince of Ravencliff, you have a chance to unite the two powers again, to shed our differences and provide a new empire."

Valen decided the truth, however blunt, was the only way to proceed. "I have no wish to marry her."

"Come here, son." His father gestured for Valen to step closer, his voice lowering to a whisper. "I, myself, had the once-in-a-lifetime chance we spoke of. I had the opportunity to remedy the broken promise, but I was young and hotheaded, and I chose selfishly. I chose otherwise, not only when I fell in love with your mother, but also when I picked my second wife. What you don't understand, my son, is I snubbed the Queen of Evenspark not once but twice, and the wrath of a woman scorned is greater than all the forces of our army put together."

Despite the admonition, Valen only found compassion for his father. "But Father, I've heard the rumors about her face..."

His father's shoulders shuddered. "I saw her once, long ago, before I met your mother."

Valen leaned in close, his interest piqued. "And?"

"I was in the royal hall in Evenspark on a diplomatic mission to meet my future bride. She came out with a retinue of handmaidens, every single one of them beautiful, but she had a thick veil on."

The king sighed, as if retelling it was painful. He took a swig of wine before continuing. "We had afternoon tea, walked in the gardens, and finally I finagled a chance to get her alone. She was standing on the balcony, wrapped in her veil and several shawls. I strolled out to meet her and asked her to show me her face. Of course, she refused."

The king looked down at the marble floor. "I told her I would understand, that physical appearance did not matter to me, it was the fate of the kingdoms that should be held above all. Moved by my depth, she showed me her face." He shrugged. "What did I know? I thought maybe she had a large nose or a wart. I was young and full of overblown ideas."

Valen took his father's hand. He surprised himself with his curiosity. "What did she look like? What is under her veils?"

Shaking his head, he hid his bearded mouth behind his hand. "No one should suffer like she has. The poor woman."

Valen wanted to probe more into his father's memories, but he knew to let it be, like so many other things that were broken and could not be mended with mere words.

His father stared at him with red-rimmed eyes. "I know I've not set the ideal example of a ruler—"

"Father, there is no need. You've done the best you could, considering the circumstances."

"No, Valen, this is important." Tears trickled down his cheeks. "You know I loved your mother deeply, more than life itself. And you know I do care for my new wife. But son, don't make the same mistakes your father made."

Valen wanted to reach out then and embrace him. Pain and pity colliding, he was overwhelmed with intricate emotions. He wanted to forgive his father for taking such a young wife, becoming a recluse in his own castle and fawning over his daughter more than his kingdom.

But suddenly the door burst open and a royal officer entered unannounced, armor clanking like pots in a kitchen. Both Valen and his father stared, speechless.

"My apologies, Your Highnesses." He was winded from running and had to gasp for breath in between each word. "But I was ordered to come right away."

"What for?" Valen's heart sank as he thought of all the awful occurrences that could warrant this type of behavior. He hoped it had nothing to do with Star.

"They've trapped him, Your Highness."

Valen paused. "Who?"

"The one who's been using that tunnel, sir. The spy."

Suddenly, Valen remembered the guards he'd posted outside the entrance to the spy tunnel in the atrium. He specifically instructed them to keep the tunnel open and watch to see who came out. He hadn't thought the invader would pop up so soon.

Valen sprinted toward the doorway, calling over his shoulder, "A conversation for later, Father. Right now I must attend to business." He didn't look back to see his father's tears and he didn't need to, for he knew they were there.

Before Valen entered the atrium, the guard signaled him to hush with one finger pressed to his lips. They sneaked in quietly and closed the door behind them. Valen recognized the guard on duty as Commander Rile's son, Allyn. The young man was anxious and alert, with his father's eagle eyes, and he whispered to Valen, "Your Highness, he's in here."

"Where?" Valen's gaze darted back and forth, searching for any sign of the intruder, but the room was unnaturally quiet. He could see the glimmer of metal armor through the ferns.

"Hiding somewhere in the shrubs. They're having trouble catching him. We've blocked off the entrance to the tunnel, but he eludes us in the greenery."

"Damn it." Valen crept forward, flanked by the guard that had rushed to fetch him. The lush vegetation stifled him, and he pushed back a palmed fern and crouched underneath the bow of a juniper. Underneath the fragrance of blossoming hyacinth was an alien stench, a pungent aroma wafting from behind the fountain. Holding up his palm, Valen told the guard to stay back and pursued the spy in ponderous steps.

Suddenly, there was a swirl of brown fabric, and the intruder jumped in front of Valen. The prince could see his long face, pointed nose and dark pupils. His hood fell back, revealing a bald head, pale as the moon and smooth as marble, as if he never saw the light of day. The man stared back at him with cold, emotionless eyes, leaving Valen with a cold stone in his stomach.

Despite the unwelcome greeting, Valen found his tongue and spoke in a hushed voice. "Who are you?"

The man dug into a pocket underneath the brown robe and brought out a shimmering globe that caught Valen's eye. Swiftly he brought up his arm and threw the glass orb to the ground in front of him. The crack left a ringing *ping* in Valen's ears. Black smoke seeped from the broken glass and masked the man's maneuvers as he disappeared into the pluming cloud.

Valen coughed and waved his arms in the fog. He heard questioning shouts around him as his guards stumbled in the haze. Confusion was everywhere—he could feel it bubbling in his thoughts, blocking out any decisive action.

"Wait! We can't lose him!" Valen shouted commands until his voice was hoarse, but when the smoke dissipated, the intruder was gone. The rock used to block the entrance to the tunnel lay askew. The intruder had managed to lift the weight by himself and escape down the tunnel under the cover of the haze.

"Should we go after him?" a guard asked, hovering over the hole in the earth.

Valen pursed his lips. He knew better. The man was probably halfway through the tunnel by now and would be entering the moors in a matter of seconds. It was too dangerous to follow him. "Inspect the tunnel. Look for any trace of his passage, but do not go beyond the fortress walls."

"Yes, sir." The guard took off a layer of his armor before lowering himself into the hole.

"And be careful." Valen handed the guard his sword. "He might still be down there."

"Yes, sir."

Valen doubted the hooded man would attack. The intruder was quick, but he hadn't had the look of a warrior or an assassin nor did he harbor the desperation of a thief. Valen paused, squinting, as he put his thoughts together like a puzzle with pieces not quite matching. The man's face surfaced in his memory: dark pupils framed by an intelligent, calculating brow. No, the intruder looked more like a philosopher, a man of learning.

Allyn spoke beside him, rousing him from his own thoughts. "The whole encounter just doesn't make sense, Your Highness. How could any man survive out there on foot?"

"I don't know." Valen picked up a piece of the shattered glass in his hands.

"If this spy tunnel's been around, then why has nothing ever been reported stolen?"

Valen wished he had the answers to give. He shook his head. "That was not his intention."

Allyn shifted nervously, eyeing the tunnel's opening. "Somehow, the fact he wasn't after gold makes me feel even more anxious."

"I know." Valen placed a hand on the young man's shoulder to reassure him. "Don't worry, we'll figure this out. In the meantime, tell your father to increase the reinforcements on the wall."

Valen's eyes scanned the trees where the man had appeared. On a branch jutting out from the thicket, he saw a torn piece of the intruder's brown robe. The fabric likely snagged on the branch. Valen plucked it from the thorny limb and held it between his fingers, smoothing over the coarse material with his fingertips. It appeared to be roughly spun wool, nothing special.

When he raised it to his nose, he sniffed the same acrid odor that had assaulted his senses moments ago when the man jumped in front of him. The smell was unlike anything Valen had ever experienced, not metallic like blood or sweat, and not sweet either. Whatever it was, Valen had the disturbing sense it was unnatural and highly toxic.

Wrapping the fabric in a handkerchief, Valen left the atrium to the attention of the guards. He took the southern stairwell to the alchemist's laboratories. The sample would be tested and, if he had luck on his side, the intruder's secret potion would be revealed. Hopefully it would shed light on the man underneath the robe and his designs.

Chapter 16

Dark Canopy

Star awoke to the slick sound of someone sharpening a knife.

She shot up from underneath her traveling blanket, realizing she lay in the cave. Her back was stiff from sleeping on stone and her stomach rumbled in disquiet, making her mood less than cheery.

Leer sat cross-legged by the fire, boiling a pot of water over the flames and cutting pieces of beef jerky in shreds before throwing them in.

"I hope that's not breakfast." Star tied her long hair back and gave him a wry look.

"I see you slept well." Leer grinned, his eyes still fixed on the food in front of him.

"When you live near the outskirts, you learn to sleep through anything."

Leer looked her up and down, skeptical. "You live by the outskirts?"

"I grew up a stone's throw away."

He seemed to regard her with a newfound level of solemn respect. His eyebrows rose quizzically. "A fellow outsider. How interesting."

Star crossed her arms. "What's so interesting about it?"

"That my cousin would be invested in someone from such…humble origins."

Insult stung her composure. Leer implied she was a poor girl nobody. She stood, blankets falling to her feet. He had her full attention. "What do you mean by that?"

"I see the way he looks at you." Leer smiled, but his lips held no happiness. "Why do you think he let me go, made me ride to my death, perhaps, in order to keep you safe?"

"It wasn't for that reason at all." Star pointed a finger in his direction. "It was because he still believes in you, because he wants to repair your broken relationship. He's offering you a second chance."

"Ha." It was clear Leer didn't buy into her philosophy and it vexed Star as if she stood before a forbidden threshold she could not cross.

She decided she was going to settle Leer's questionable trustworthiness once and for all. It hung in the air between them like a dead skunk, inhibiting their conversation from the start of the journey. Kicking her blankets out of the way, she crouched directly in front of him, staring until his eyes met her own.

"He believed your claim. He had faith you were going to report the assassination when it was time." She searched the sharp lines of his face for any sign of truth or deception, but found only amusement flickering in his eyes, like each orb held a small fire of its own.

His gaze followed the curve of her cheek, ending on a stray strand of iridescent hair hanging below her chin. He abandoned his task of cutting up meat. "And do you?"

In the heat of the moment, Star had pushed her face right in front of his, and now she suddenly felt too close. She could smell his tangy scent of pine mixed with smoke. "Do I what?"

"Do you believe that I'm a killer or a prince in shining armor?"

His face drew her in, as if an invisible force pulled her forward. It would only take a slight movement to touch her lips to his and that thought scared her more than any Elyndra or dead journeyman.

She sniffed and turned away to tend to Windracer. "I don't think you're either." As she retreated deeper into the cave, she could hear him laughing lightly over the crackling morning fire. The mystery of Leer was going to be hard to unravel. But she was up for the challenge.

* * * *

They rode relentlessly throughout the day. The countryside grew eerie and ill-omened as the mist coalesced around them, thickening with each pace. Star felt like a wraith riding to the end of the world, where the spirit realm met those who passed from life to death.

A dark presence loomed on the horizon in an ocean of black shadows, growing ever vaster as they rode to meet their destiny. Soon, Star could make out vague shapes forming from the mass. At first they looked uncannily like grasping arms and groping fingers protruding from a writhing ball of lost souls, but as she rode closer, she recognized scraggly branches and tattered leaves. Thorny brambles grew in this part of the land, as if it suffered a suffocating existence in the dense mist. Star wondered if any sunlight was able to filter through at all.

They approached the edge of a colossal forest thick with Blackwood. The trees hung over them, spilling onto the land like strewn towers.

Heavy mist dampened the earth and the horses slowed their pace, treading carefully as the muck sucked down their hooves.

Star could barely see the tip of Leer's broad nose in the shaded hood of his riding cloak. "I wonder if any journeymen have made it this far."

Leer reined in Wildfire and turned in her direction. He had a crazy spark in his eye, a craving for adventure. "We shall see. I've never heard such a forest described."

"It's hideous. The trees look like the stuff of nightmares."

"Funny. I thought they were picturesque."

Star shot Leer a confused look before she realized he was joking. She rolled her eyes and continued without comment, wondering why he found her and their situation so amusing. As she rode on, she found herself smiling and realized his teasing jabs lifted her spirits, lightening the mood in this wild and desolate region.

Their horses picked their way through the underbrush and upturned roots as Star and Leer pushed dangling moss aside to pass through. Fervent life covered the forest floor. Ferns, vines, shrubs and the beginnings of new trees worked their way through the mist to claim the trickling light.

Star grew frustrated as a tangled branch caught Windracer's hoof. "We're moving so slowly. We're easy targets."

She moved to dismount, but Leer held up his hand and stalled her. "I'll get the snag."

"If the Elyndra don't get us first." She tried to hide her shiver from Leer.

Leer slid off Wildfire and freed the hoof. "Don't worry. I don't think the beasts can penetrate the canopy."

Although Leer had a point, Star hoped they didn't have to test his theory. At least the Elyndra couldn't spy on them from above, and they would have a warning if one did try to break through. The broken branches alone would make enough of a ruckus to wake them from a coma.

When the woods grew dark, they made camp underneath the bows of an immense Blackwood larger than Star's house in the outskirts and probably older than Star's great-grandparents.

Although Leer spoke seldom if at all, Star wanted something to fill the silence as they spread their blankets by the fire. The woods around them trembled in the wind, the bows creaking as though they spoke a warning. Star positioned her bedspread close to the fire's light.

"It's strange." Leer smoothed his blanket across a level patch of forest floor. "Such a large and fertile forest, and no signs of life other than trees."

"What do you suppose?"

"I don't know. I'm not a man of learning like your Prince Valen." Leer threw a stick into the fire and the flames licked higher.

"He's not my prince," Star was quick to answer, taking his bait before she even knew that's what it was.

"Really?" Leer poked the flames and settled onto his blanket, crossing his legs.

"I live in Evenspark and answer to our queen." The conversation made her uncomfortable. Star's feelings for Valen were all tangled up, and she wasn't about to unravel them right here in front of Leer. She rose to her feet and looked for something to do in order to hide her blush of feelings. Windracer was her best bet. The mare's hooves were gummed with muddied earth from the long day's journey. Star brought out the blunt end of her dagger and picked at the crusted hooves, taking out her frustration on the impacted grime.

"I didn't mean you follow him as your prince."

Star knew how he'd meant it. She refused to comment further and a heavy silence fell on their camp, filled with intermittent chinks as Star worked the day's ride out of Windracer's hooves.

"You love him, don't you?"

Star pretended to be highly involved with a certain stubborn clump of sod. "I don't understand where you get your crazy ideas, but the feelings I have for Prince Valen are admiration and respect and nothing else."

"Oh, is that right?" Sarcasm danced in Leer's words. "Then prove it. If you don't love Valen, then come over here and kiss me."

Star was shocked beyond words. No man had ever asked her for a kiss and in such an utterly scoundrel manner. "Kissing you is the most ridiculous thing I've ever heard. It wouldn't prove anything."

"Maybe I'll just have to come over there and kiss you myself."

Star dropped Windracer's hoof and glared. "You take one step toward me and you're a dead man. You know better than to attack a messenger."

Leer laughed lightly. "You forget, I was a messenger myself."

She drew her arm back to fling her dagger at the tree behind him as a warning when a strange sound came from the woods behind them. It was a sickly sucking noise, like a pig in a water trough. The leaves rustled. Suddenly Leer wasn't the enemy after all.

"What is it?" Star whispered, stepping closer to the fire.

Another noise erupted from a different direction. Whatever it was, there were more of them around. Windracer and Wildfire danced around in skittish steps, tied to the limb of the Blackwood. Star wondered if it was more dangerous to keep them there or let them run free. At least if something happened to her or Leer, the horses would be able to get away.

Dagger in hand, Leer was on his feet before Star could turn her head. He put a finger to his lips. Star realized with dreadful shock he was going into the woods to find out.

"No!" She reached out her arm to stop him. "Don't be stupid."

Leer waved her back. "Calm down."

The rustling surrounded them. The things in the woods outnumbered them and they were closing in. Star followed behind Leer, circling to keep all sides guarded. The sucking noises rang out into the night like the perverse grunts of an oversized boar. They were getting louder with each racing heartbeat.

Before Leer could enter the forest, the woods parted behind them. Star and Leer turned around just as a pale mass of skin, larger than Windracer, squirmed through the woods on a multitude of small hairy legs and into their camp. Two large antennae spread out like arms, feeling around. When the antennae touched the heat of the fire, the monster retreated, directing the large body back into the woods.

"The fire!" Star yelled. "Get as close to it as possible." She could tell he wanted to fight but kept him back with a firm grip on his arm. They stood, back to back, the heat from Leer's body a steady reassurance.

"Whatever you do, don't attack. I don't want to know what defensive techniques it's acquired through evolution." She didn't like the look of the pin-like bristles on its body. One strike and they could be poisonous.

One by one, the giant caterpillars emerged from the forest, halting precariously at the edge of the fire's warmth. Their myriad legs twitched in the firelight. Star could see two sharp and thorny protrusions coming from either side of their mouths. They looked like they could snap her leg with one clutch.

"I think the smoke and heat confuses them," Leer said under his breath.

"Let's stay right here until they go away." Star stared incredulously at the monstrosities. The absurdity of being surrounded by caterpillar-like beasts was like some children's nightmare coming true before her eyes. "Where do you think they come from anyways?"

Leer gestured with a nod of his head to the woods looming in front of them. "The north." He curled his lips in a rare half smile. "Right where we're headed."

"Great." Star watched as the slimy slugs retreated back into the darkness of the forest. "I can't wait."

Leer gazed wistfully into the night canopy above. His words were melancholic, tinted with slight amusement. "And the night was going so well…"

Chapter 17

Repellent

Valen stared through green glowing vials, waiting patiently as Odious, the kingdom's chief alchemist, studied the fabric sample through multiple lenses attached to his spectacles. Bubbling potions and steaming liquids cluttered the tables of the laboratory, and misty cauldrons and caged rodents lay sprawled on the floor. Entombed in the far reaches of the castle, the room was lit by a series of torches on the far wall, their flickering light casting all manner of sinister shadows on tables strewn with old rolls of parchment and silver tools of measurement and dissection. The room reminded Valen of a torture chamber mixed with a mad scientist's laboratory and never failed to send a shiver down his neck.

"It appears to be simple wool fabric, scented with a substance alkaline in nature." Odious's gaze was glued to the magnifying glass. Various experiments lay scattered around him in shallow glass dishes, displayed like an exotic feast for mice.

Indeed, Valen thought with mild disgust, the mice would come later, subjected to the dishes for clinical purposes. He stifled a shudder and walked over to the far side of the table where a lizard coiled around a broken tree limb, a slender chain clasped around its neck.

"Yes, but do you have any guess what it does?" Valen took a piece of crumb from a discarded meal left on a platter by the door and held it between the bars of a magpie's cage. The bird hopped hesitantly toward his fingers, turning a wary black eye in his direction.

"It's not for stealth, that's for sure. You can smell it five feet away." Odious finally looked up at Valen. "And Crayraven won't eat from anyone's hands, so you can just give up now."

"But why would the man spray it all over his cloak?" Valen ignored the suggestion about the bird. His fingers held the crumb steady and patiently as he whistled a gentle tune. It hopped closer and pivoted its feathery head in a questioning glance but did not reach for the crumb.

"It's got to be for some kind of protection, maybe against water damage or wind."

"Why sacrifice stealth to ensure the life of a cloak? It's more important than mere weather protection."

"I'm not certain yet. Your theory must be tested."

Before Valen could stop him, Odious held the clothing scrap to a caged rabbit. "What are you doing?" Valen raised his voice in alarm. "It may be poisonous."

"I'm doing my job." Odious unbolted the cage door.

Valen watched with horror as the furry angora hopped close to the fabric. It took one sniff, identified it as nonfood and disregarded Odious's offering like old news. Valen realized he was holding his breath and let out a sigh of relief. He had no stomach for experimentation.

Meanwhile, the magpie inched closer to the bread crumb resting in Valen's fingertips.

"It has no effect on mammals." Odious seemed baffled. "And with enough water, it washes away."

The bird took the final hop to Valen's fingertips, accepting the crumb with a gentle peck. A rush of success flooded his senses. If a bird could trust him, then he might be able to win the hearts of his countrymen after all. He looked to Odious with a grin, but the alchemist was still enthralled with the fabric, this time rubbing it on a piece of parchment, like it held some secret message.

As he waited, Valen watched as gray and white moths flitted around the flaming torches at the opposite end of the room. It was almost as if the moths teased death. Some flew directly into the fire, their powdery wings consumed in seconds. Valen wondered why the moths were captivated by the object causing their demise. Why did their distant relatives, the Elyndra, possess the intelligence to avoid the flames when their smaller cousins did not?

Suddenly Valen had an idea. Walking across the room, he took the piece of fabric from Odious's eager fingertips, ignoring his questioning complaints, and held it to the hovering moths. Instantly, they flittered away to the far reaches of the cobwebbed ceiling.

"That's it!" Valen held the fabric like a prize. "It's a repellent of some sort. It keeps the Elyndra away."

"That's how the intruder navigates the walls outside the fortress unharmed. The substance repels them. But why?" Odious asked, more rhetorically. "What is it about the odor they disfavor so vehemently?"

"Why is not the most important question right now." Valen searched Odious's eyes with hope. "What I want to know is can you copy it?"

Suddenly, a horn sounded down the echoing halls leading throughout the castle. It was a long wailing call, followed by two short utterances. Seconds later it was repeated again.

Odious walked toward the hall to peek his head out. "What is going on?"

"It is a warning signal." Valen draped the cloak over a chair, his thoughts turning to the guards stationed on the wall. He hoped they were prepared.

The alchemist walked toward the door to check out the situation, and Valen ran over to pull him back. "Listen to me, this is crucial." Valen's grip tightened on his arm. "Stay inside and bolt your door. We're going to need as many odor-soaked cloaks as possible. Get to work on reproducing that repellent."

"But why?"

Valen's eyes rose to the ceiling, looking beyond the castle walls. He let the old man go as his hand moved instinctively toward the hilt of his sword. "That is a distinctive alarm. The mist is rising."

* * * *

People scattering in alarm clogged the streets of Ravencliff. Valen had to fight his way to the battlements. There was chaos everywhere and so many people needing help.

Valen tripped over a young, drunk squire. The man looked up groggily before recognizing the Prince of Ravencliff. "Your Highness, my apologies…"

"Not now." Valen waved him back as he stood. "Get up and get under cover. There isn't much time."

The squire froze, suddenly sobered with shock and disbelief.

"Go." Valen pulled him to his feet. "Get yourself somewhere safe."

Valen turned and heard a young girl's screams rise up from the shouts to hide and the whinnies of finicky horses. He saw a small, frumpy street urchin left alone in the marketplace holding a grimy doll in one hand, the other dragging a moth-eaten shawl on the ground.

As Valen propelled himself through the crowd to reach her, he was almost hit by a carriage as the horses skittered back and forth, trying to avoid crashing. Another carriage rammed into a vendor's stand, sending apples flying past his head. Valen finally reached the girl and kneeled down to talk with her. "Where is your mother?"

The girl choked on sobs. Her tear-stained face told him she'd been crying for a long time now and her body shook with exhaustion. She looked at him as if he were trying to trick her and refused to answer, shaking her head.

There was no time for polite explanations. Valen snatched her up in both arms and ran to the healer's quarters underneath the parapets. The woman in white robes looked up from her bundle of bottles and vials, startled at the sight of the prince with a grubby rascal from the street.

"Please take her. She's lost her mother." He handed the girl over to the older woman. He looked at the others in the room. "And the rest of you— be prepared. War is upon us and your skills will be needed."

When he finally reached the top of the parapets, the soldiers had already begun piling up sandbags on top of the steep wall. The commander-in-chief, Stoughton Rile, met him halfway, bowing ceremoniously despite the chaos that surged behind him. "Your Highness."

Valen ignored his formalities. "How far?"

His answer came with one look over the commander's shoulders. The mist seeped through cracks in the sandbags, surpassing the fortress walls.

"We are keeping it at bay, Your Highness." Rile defended his station with confidence. "Only small tendrils are creeping through. I have every man that can shoot an arrow equipped and ready to fire."

For Valen, that wasn't enough. "Is it still rising or has it stopped?"

The commander squinted, looking back over his shoulder. "Hard to say."

A sudden gust of air threw Valen's hair back from his forehead and sent his cloak whipping behind him. Valen turned to the north. The mist traveled fast, aided by the unseasonable wind. Ladders teetered in the raging gale as the lookouts climbed with bows in hand to keep abreast of the growing wall. Valen ran to steady one ladder as an archer reached the top. The young man's face was hardened for the battle, but Valen saw fear, raw and untamed, shine in his eyes.

Valen didn't realize that his grip was so fierce until someone took his place holding the ladder. Rubbing the splintered palms of his hands, he surveyed the battlements with an uneasy estimation. In that moment, the entire fortress was a precarious barricade. Suddenly Star's journey no longer seemed so impulsive and farfetched. He wished he'd supported her with his entire heart, but his heart was not his to give away. It belonged to the throne.

With a sting of regret, he realized if he had extended more encouragement, she might have spoken to him more openly before she left. Now he wondered if he'd ever get another chance to speak to her at all.

Valen reached into the deep folds of his cape and clutched the letter she'd brought to him, as if the paper could somehow tie him back to her. He pleaded with the gods to protect her not only for his own selfish desires, but for the good of the kingdom. Every life in Ravencliff dangled from the thread of her success.

Chapter 18

Journey's End

Star and Leer broke free of the fog-smothered forest the next day. Although the giant caterpillars had vanished into the misted limbs like vipers into burrowed holes, neither of them could sleep. Restless from the night's visitation, they felt an urge to press on before the first rays of dawn graced the horizon. It would be better to face the end of the forest in broad daylight and get a head start on whatever awaited them at the mist's end.

The mist carried on, thick as ever, a milky film blurring their eyes and bogging down their cloaks with dankness. It gushed from the north like it overflowed from a primordial waterfall standing sentinel at the tundra's end.

During the course of the forest, the edge of mountains slowly receded into foothills and tapered away into a desolate hinterland of barren plateaus at the forest's perimeter. Now there was nowhere to hide.

"Leer, what if I was wrong?" Star asked softly as they peered through the last trunks of trees into nothingness. "What if the mist just keeps getting thicker?"

Leer turned and Star could see half his face underneath his hood. His expression was calm as ever. "No. Everything has an end." He winked, surprising Star yet again. "Come on, Miss Doom, let's settle down, let our horses rest and eat something before we race out there without cover."

Leer's words loosened the clench in her heart and she smiled to herself, surprised that he had so much power over her mood. She knew he was right. They would need every second of energy to keep their pace fast enough and they didn't know how long the expanse ran. Although Leer believed in her, Star's own doubts were festering.

They made a makeshift camp at the edge of the forest. Leer started a fire to cook food and ward off the giant caterpillars should they come back. Trying to get her mind off the impending race ahead of them, Star turned to Leer with a question that had simmered in her thoughts for some time. "Leer, why did you quit the Interkingdom Carriers?"

He looked up from his boiling concoction of stew with amusement in his eyes. Star knew he was flattered by her interest in his past. After a moment of reflection, the lines on his strong-boned face hardened. "Too much corruption."

Star was shocked. She thought it might have been about his own negligence, the harsh schedule, any number of things, but not that. "I didn't think I would, but I completely understand."

Leer nodded. "Probably so."

She picked up a twig and broke it between her fingers. "I could complain for days about my experience with corruption. Favors for the gentry, free letters getting smuggled in. Heck, I was even replaced with someone who could be 'more diplomatic,' if you catch the drift."

"If you are here now, what happened to your replacement?" Leer didn't ask many questions, so Star knew she'd caught his attention.

"Dead. I found only a pool of her blood."

Leer laughed lightly. "Serves her right."

"Leer!" Star was shocked. It was such a dastardly reply, and disrespectful of the dead, but a part of her liked the fact that he was so willing to stand up for her and take her side. An enemy of hers was an enemy of his. She shook her head. "To think we've encountered the same trials in each of our lives. I used to love my job. Besides my family, it was all I had—a summation of all my accomplishments and hard work. But after the incident with the replacement and your letter, I've felt like quitting as well…"

A sly smile spread over Leer's lips. "Despite our differences in opinion, you and I are much the same."

Star sat back, studying the lines in his face and wondering if he was right. He had an easiness to his personality that Valen lacked, a calm, underlying trust that he controlled his own destiny, coupled with an acceptance of the inevitability of certain things. He calmed the nervous anxiety bubbling through her and she found herself glad he sat with her in this nightmarish land.

* * * *

After sipping Leer's motley stew made from their dwindling provisions and foraged food, they packed and prepared the horses for the final race to the finish line. Both Star and Leer knew they were drawing closer to something big and powerful. Whether it was a force they could reckon with was another matter.

Star reigned in Windracer at the forest's edge, a vast plain spreading out before them. "So here we are at the end of the world."

"Indeed." Leer's eyes grew mischievous. "You are quite the adventurer, Miss Moonshine."

"And you are quite the partner." Star could feel her cheeks burning so hot she thought the mist would sizzle out around her face. She turned her head away, ashamed of the feelings she developed for Valen's supposed assassin. In fact, she hadn't thought much about Valen the past few days.

They took off with a rustle of leaves, leaving the canopy's cover and entering the unknown.

The smooth terrain allowed for swift riding. Star felt as though she careened across the slick surface of a frozen lake. They needed to maintain speed to keep the Elyndra at bay. Every time Star chanced a brave look at the sky, she saw shapes moving above her head, giant shadows of wings soaring through the mist as the beasts cluttered the sky. One misstep and they'd be picked off the ground like mice.

At first Star thought she imagined it, but with every racing hoofbeat, the mist seemed to be thinning as if the ground soaked it up. Star's hopes rose. Maybe they'd found the mist's end after all.

Leer raised a hand to his brow and squinted against the mist. His features turned from mild interest to horror. "Stop!" He reined in Wildfire. "Stop Windracer now!"

Star couldn't imagine standing still with the Elyndra hovering. "But—"

All of a sudden, Leer veered in her direction. Wildfire forced Windracer to lurch directly to the left to avoid colliding in a tangle of legs.

"What are you doing?" Star fought the pull of gravity and the knot of reins. "You'll get us both killed!" Windracer leaned into the fall, regained balance and straightened, trained from years of riding in the stadium amongst the other foolhardy contestants where a random blow to the side was common.

When Star regained control over Windracer, she realized Leer herded her away from the line of thinning mist up ahead. A few feet further, the mist disappeared over the edge of a deadly steep canyon lining the horizon. If Leer hadn't ascertained the reason why the mist thinned, they both would have ridden to their deaths, plummeting over the edge with no warning. Star realized he'd just saved both of their lives.

Leer was beginning to look more like a hero than a criminal. That thought brought along others like it, and Star realized that her feelings for Leer changed the way she thought of Valen. He spoke of his cousin as a selfish criminal, and Leer was more of a savior in disguise.

"Over there," he shouted over his shoulder. "I see a way down."

Star followed Leer to the cliff's edge where the ridges of rock separated, revealing a rocky slope lining the canyon wall. Shivers tickled her back, making the hair on her neck stand on end. "Are you sure you want to go down?"

"Seems like there's nowhere else to go. Besides, I have a feeling this path will take us to some answers."

"You mean because it looks like someone carved it into the canyon?"

Leer's eyes narrowed. "Exactly."

* * * *

Jagged rocks made the footing treacherous. Dizziness overtook her senses each time she looked over the ledge to the depths of shadows taking refuge below the line of mist. To Star's relief, no Elyndra chanced a flight into the steep canyon. She and Leer inched down the steep incline, tugging their horses behind them, careful not to kick a stray rock over the ledge. It would be foolish to alert whoever resided down in the canyon. Theirs was an uninvited and probably unwelcome visit.

Star shook her head, trying to make sense of a distant throbbing in her eardrums.

"Flies getting to you?" Leer grinned.

"No. There's a weird sound ringing in my ears, like the distant buzzing of a giant wasp. Can't you hear it?"

Leer tilted his head into the breeze, the hood of his cloak brushing against the three-day stubble on his cheeks. "Hearing is not my strongest sense."

"What is your advantage?" Star hoped to prolong the conversation and get her mind off the relentless hum.

"Sight. Not only of physical objects, but intentions and emotions."

His answer unnerved her, his words stripping her cool facade, as if he could see her innermost desires and needs. Part of her wanted to ask him, "What do you see when you look at me?" She looked back at the path meandering in front of them, turning her back to Leer so he couldn't see the rush of blood flood her face.

The humming grew louder near the bottom of the canyon as they descended. It vibrated inside her like an alien song from another land. Star felt an unnatural force surrounding the place and had to convince herself to continue down into the depths.

"Look." Leer pointed to the canyon floor.

Star strained her eyes. If she concentrated, she could just make out strange bumps resting at the base of the gorge, like the backs of giants wrapped in quilts, their forms rising and falling in deep slumber.

"What are they?" she whispered, afraid to rouse the strange beings from their hibernation.

"It seems to me," Leer guessed under his breath, "they are Elyndra in an early stage of life."

"No." Star stopped in her tracks, raising her hand to her mouth in disbelief. "It can't be." But the closer she looked, the more the wrapped objects seemed like cocoons writhing with black legs inside. Her goals seemed to materialize in front of her. They'd succeeded in at least one aspect of the quest: they'd found the Elyndra's lair and their offspring.

Leer stepped toward her, his head above hers, looking down so that his breath moved strands of her hair. "You did it, Star. You found what you were looking for."

A sudden rush of camaraderie rose up inside her. "We did it."

He shook his head. "All I did was make sure you didn't do anything foolish."

Star's eyes crinkled in skepticism. "Isn't that the other way around?"

But the sight before them distracted Leer, his eyes returning to the alien bodies spread below.

Star squinted. "What is it?"

"There are shapes moving in the mist." Her hand shot immediately to the torch at her side, but Leer held her back. "They're not big enough to be Elyndra. In fact, they look like people." Leer's mouth twitched in disgust, his jaw clenching.

Star tugged on Windracer, turning around. "Then we must save them!"

Again Leer held her back, this time grabbing her arm like he did that fateful night she brought him Zetta's letter. She did not fight back but let him hold her in place. Rogue that he was, he had gained a certain measure of her trust.

"You don't understand." Leer locked eyes with her own, his gaze intense as fire. "They seem to be caring for the cocoons."

"What?" Star tried to make sense of his words, but no logic came. "Why would people be helping the awful monstrosities? You must be mistaken."

Leer frowned as though he wished he was wrong.

Star leaned forward over the ledge, relying on Leer's solid grip of her arm. She looked down into the depths of the mist, thinking she saw thin figures waver in and out of the haze, but the people were too far away and her eyes blurred. "Do they walk below that mountain?"

"Wait." Leer peered over the ledge in silence. When he did speak, his voice held awe laced with a current of deep dismay. "That's not a mountain. It's a machine."

"It can't be. It's too big." But somehow the way the surface caught the faint rays of sun was unnatural, like the exterior was slick with oil and paint. Star's stomach lurched with the sheer thought of it.

"That's not all." Leer pointed to the apex of the monolithic structure. "Look."

Star gazed up, her hood falling behind her shoulders, and beheld the root of all their fears. A hideous concoction of terror blew its twisted whimsy over the countryside like foul breath. White smog poured out from its summit, the device churning it out with glee.

Star stumbled back. "It's a mist-making machine."

Her mind flooded with complex emotions. Every event in her life seemed to bring her to this culminating moment, this intended purpose, as if she was predestined to be its destroyer. An iron edge tinged her voice. "I'm going to stop it."

"Hold your horses, Miss Save the World." Leer put both hands on her shoulders. "First we have to find a way past them." He pointed back behind his shoulder. "Not an easy task, I'm sure."

Star squirmed with frustration. She was so close and yet her goal seemed more far away than it had ever been. It was two of them against an entire sleeping army and who knew how many caretakers. Star stifled her urge to rush down there and destroy the machine right then and there as she tore her eyes away from the hideous scene to face Leer, feeling lost. "What do we do?"

"Find a hiding place first, that's for sure." Leer cast a stray look over his shoulder. "One big enough to hold two horses. Then we craft a plan."

Chapter 19

Sacrifice

They found a crack in the rock surface toward the bottom of the incline. Leer investigated first, disappearing into the darkness with a match set aflame. Star pulled the horses close to the wall, hoping the thickness of the mist hid their outlines. For once, the blurry substance was an aid, not a hindrance.

The figures below continued to survey the cocoons, walking between the lines of bodies in a slow, methodical manner. They didn't seem too concerned with the sky or the trail leading up toward the plateau.

Leer emerged a few minutes later. "It's safe. And there's enough room for both horses."

Star sighed, relieved. "Good. I don't know how often those robed men come up this incline, but I don't want to be in plain sight when they do."

The horses struggled as they led them through the narrow crevice of stone. Finicky as they already were, the claustrophobic space seemed to unnerve them even more. Star was relieved when it opened to a larger cave and a pool of trickling rain water.

They made camp as best they could, but neither Star nor Leer had a stomach for food. After tending to the horses, Star slumped against the stone wall as Leer returned from surveying the grounds below.

"What did you see?"

Leer shrugged. "More of the same. I estimate fifty or so workers and a hundred sleeping Elyndra."

Star shook her head. Everything she saw questioned her own sense of reason and logic and her view of the world.

Leer stood beside her, raising a hand above the rock to lean in by her face. "What's the matter?"

"I don't understand who they are. I know no one from either Ravencliff or Evenspark would live in such a place, tending to such horrible creations.

How could we have lived so long near them and never know who they are?"

"Seems to me they didn't want to be found."

Star guessed Leer was not a philosopher but she had to vent her frustrations. "Why do they do such things? Why are they here?"

Leer brought his hand down, resting it on her shoulder. The gesture was oddly comforting in such a harsh, cold place at the end of the world as they knew it. "I don't know, but you're right. They must be stopped. And I promise I'll help you succeed."

The intensity of Leer's words and his steady gaze made Star blush. It was not a time for such feelings, nor the place or the person with whom to start a lasting romance. Star picked up a rock to hide her sudden rush of emotion and squeezed her hand around it. "The odds aren't favorable."

Leer's eyebrows quirked in a challenge. "The odds are never good."

Star was in no mood for jests and spoke through clenched teeth. "I need to get close enough to destroy the machine undetected and I need time to find out how to do it, to look for a weakness."

Leer's eyes flickered to the cavern entrance and back. Star knew he weighed the options like a predator caught in a cage. His words were dire, his tone dead. "We can't stay here forever."

"So what do we do? Ride home in retreat?" Star shook her head. "There's no way we can march an army through that forest, never mind through the open mist, and no one can ride as fast as we can. The mist is rising each day. It has to be done now." She felt so anxious and frustrated she thought her heart would burst. She squeezed her hands together until the tips of her fingers swelled with uncirculated blood.

Leer, on the other hand, was stoic and contemplative. He sat next to her, resting his back against the cavern wall. "There is only one way."

Star swished her head toward him, white hair flinging against his chest. "And what is that?"

"I ride out toward the field of cocoons and set them on fire, causing a ruckus to draw the workers away. You sneak into the machine and destroy it."

"But that's too dangerous. It's suicide. There's no way you can make it back to the ridge. If you succeed, it will blossom to a blazing inferno, and if they catch you—"

"How do you know this is the only way out?" Leer countered, but his words were empty. Both of them knew of the slim probability.

"No." Star jutted out her chin. "I won't do it."

Leer spread his hands out, palms up. "It's the only way."

She locked her gaze with his. "We ride together."

His eyes widened. "Then we both die."

Star turned away, her cheeks hot with tears. "I can't...I can't let you go."

Leer sat forward, his body only inches from her own. "And why is that? We both know I was a dead man back in Ravencliff." He reached across the distance between them and took her chin in his fingertips, raising her face to look him in the eye. "Why's it so hard to let me go now?"

Star felt a rush of emotion at the touch. Leer was such a mystery to her, all rough around the edges but passionate and soft at the core. The one thing she was certain of was that he would never kill Valen. "Because I know you're innocent."

He leaned in so close his breath fell on her lips. "And is that all?"

Star pulled her head back from his hand. She wasn't ready to deal with her rising emotions head on. "Isn't that enough of a reason right there?"

Leer looked away, disappointed. "It's getting late. Let's try to get some sleep. We have a big day ahead of us tomorrow."

Unable to come to any agreement on the plan, Star and Leer rolled themselves up in their travel blankets and the cave fell silent. Star drifted off to sleep as night closed in. Her dreams were feverish, her mind ranting about secret passages and wings, sleeping monsters and ominous machines. In each dream, she battled hard and lost every situation, leading to only one possible outcome—their own demise.

* * * *

When Star woke, light filtered from the crack in the stone face. The mist had crept into their hiding place during the night and it gathered around her sleeping form, watching, waiting and biding its time. Star waved it back, swinging her arms in front of her face until the substance thinned and she could see the rest of the cave.

Windracer and Wildfire slept soundly, unmoving. But Leer was gone. She shot up from her travel blanket, eyes scanning the cavern back and forth. Stupid rogue! Star cursed under her breath. Had he already gone without her? Still numb from restless sleep and her legs full of anxious energy, Star strode to the cavern entrance to have a look for herself.

On her way, she bumped into a dark figure and almost screamed. The man held her close and put a gentle hand over her mouth. It was Leer. "Shh, let's go back inside."

"What were you doing out there?" Star felt like a mother scolding her son. "You could have been killed!"

Leer smirked. "I was scouting, looking for the best possible way down and across the cocoons."

"You're not going out there by yourself again."

But Leer seemed like he wasn't listening. He went straight to Wildfire, fastening the reins on tight. When he spoke next, his words were heavy and solemn. "All my life, I blamed myself for Valen's mother's death." He adjusted the stirrups and Star stood shocked and unable to move. Leer meant to tell her the truth. "I felt undeserving of his good will." He turned to face her. "But now I can make it up to him, to the entire population of Ravencliff."

Star gritted her teeth. "What do you mean?"

"I'm going to create the distraction you need in order to break that hideous machine. Then the rest is up to you, Star. Destroy that contraption, make it back to Ravencliff and marry Prince Valen." Leer gave her a smile more wistful than anything else. "It's a lot on your shoulders, but I know you can do it. All you need is time and a decent diversion."

Star stumbled forward, barely able to speak. "No."

But Leer's resolution was much stronger than her meager attempt to stop him. He walked to meet her, pulling Wildfire behind him. "The truth is, I don't know who was behind the assassination attempt. I was involved to try to find out and clear my name and reputation with Valen forever. You caught me before I was able to pinpoint the person at the top of the chain of command."

Star went to speak but Leer held a finger to her lips. "That's all right. This has worked out much better. Not only will I be able to help with this threat to Ravencliff, but I'll take as many of those awful beasts with me as I can."

She could not hold back the tears flowing in a stream down her cheeks. She knew he had made up his mind long before she could talk him out of it, but she had to try to stop him. "Fallon, don't do it." Her professional demeanor had been a barrier she'd held up the entire journey, and now it melted away like ice in the summer sun.

Leer's eyes brightened when she said his first name. "It is the only way." He bent down and kissed the hot tears on her face before touching his lips to her own. His hand traveled up her neck to cradle her head as they stood there together, heated bodies pressing close. His arms surrounded her and for a moment she forgot all about the Elyndra, Ravencliff and even Valen.

Then he tore himself away. Before Star could react, Leer exited the cave, pulling Wildfire behind. Her hand reached for his cloak, but her fingers closed on thin air. She ran after him, but it was too late. After all, Leer had been a messenger himself, and he rode faster than her by a landslide.

Shaking, she ran back into the cave and jumped on Windracer. She would not fail him, and he would not die in vain. If she had anything to do about it, he would not die at all.

Chapter 20

Promise

"Funny thing, I've always secretly thought of the mist as a blessing."

Commander Rile stood over the prince with concern sketched in his timeworn features. For Valen, it seemed time had stopped once Star and Leer left only a few days ago. He'd been staring into the mist for hours, his eyes glossed over with opaque shadows and wispy tendrils. The familiar sound of a human voice called him away from the dreamscape, calming his frayed nerves.

"You see, it's the one thing holding back Evenspark's army and that dreaded, disfigured queen's foul rage."

The hoarseness of his tone surprised Valen. "Sometimes an old enemy is a friend in disguise."

Just like Leer. The intent of the statement he'd said out loud hit him hard and he swayed back, bracing himself against the stone wall. He realized that he did still have love for Leer. He'd sent the two people he cared about the most into the valley of the beasts. His concern weighed his features down and Commander Rile crouched beside him, kneeling at his feet.

"You've been at watch far longer than your shift, my prince."

Valen rubbed his temples. "I'm not going down."

"Forgive me, Your Highness, but you must rest some time."

Valen dismissed him with a wave. "No. Not until this threat is gone." He squinted, looking back over the battlements like a madman. "Not until she comes back."

The commander looked at him, confused. "Who, Your Highness?"

Although he'd not meant to, Valen had voiced his last thought out loud. At this point, he didn't care what gossip ran amuck within Ravencliff's walls. He would start following his heart, whether it was the right thing to do or not.

"The messenger. She's going to save us all." Valen focused back on the foggy nothingness, but his thoughts returned to the last conversation he'd had with Star at the gate. He'd wanted to say so much, and yet all he could do was stand by when she left without another word. How he'd cursed his inaction in the days since. "Commander, I love her."

Valen turned back but Commander Rile was gone. The prince looked down the length of the battlements in both directions but the commander had disappeared. In fact, eerily enough, Valen was the only one on duty.

"It can't be. My men would not abandon their posts…"

Suddenly he felt a chill breeze on his back and his body prickled with goose bumps, the hair on his arms standing on end. In a split second, he felt a whish of air over his head. He ducked impulsively, falling onto his back. An Elyndra swooped from the mist above his head, legs grasping frantically for his body. It had missed in the initial assault, but hovered in the open air above him, boldly crossing the fortress's walls.

Valen struggled, squirming underneath the clawed talons. He managed to get hold of his sword and swung it out of the sheath. With a clang, the metal blade hit one of the legs, but it ricocheted off the hard carapace and the beast pressed on. He wondered how the beast had stolen the commander. These days, everything happened so fast and he wasn't prepared for any of it. His mind roamed the land of daydreams instead.

He rolled out of its grasp and ducked underneath an old cannon that hadn't been used in years. He watched as the luminescent beast landed on the stone of the battlements, batting its silvery wings. Two large antennae explored the air around it, searching for its lost quarry. The beast was massive, its wingspan larger than two wagons put together, and Valen wondered how Star had managed to kill one all by herself, hanging from a rope, of all places.

Then he remembered Star telling him the Elyndra feared fire. Holding his breath and digging in his coat pocket, Valen found a match.

A bag of sand rested underneath the cannon. Valen emptied the bag silently and tied the sack around the tip of his sword. Meanwhile, the Elyndra jittered and ticked above him, exploring the structure of the wall. Valen struck the match and lit the sack, watching it spark with flame.

The heat of the fire alerted the Elyndra and it spun around in his direction, antennae raised. Valen thrust the sword into its wing and the flames caught and spread. It tried to fly, propelling itself into the air, but the blaze erupted on both wings. The beast tilted and fell over the side of the fortress to the ground below in a ball of fire.

Valen had a moment of triumph followed by a stinging realization of sheer terror: his side of the fortress was probably not the only one under attack. There would be more of them to come, possibly in greater numbers.

Scrambling down the length of the battlements to the main turret, Valen found the warning horn abandoned at the foot of the sentry's station, sprinkled with drops of blood. The beasts had picked the watch tower guards off first, and then turned to the lookout guards on the parapet.

Wiping the horn on his coat, Valen watched for signs of other beasts. Taking a deep breath, he put his lips to the mouthpiece and blew into the horn. A long, wailing sound careened through the upper parapet. Although he was not a trained bugler, he had played with the horns as a child and was familiar with the particular rhythm of a battle call. The pitch and tone were rough, but the expressed sentiment was clear as ever.

Just as he finished a long string of notes, Valen looked up at the sky behind him. A wave of dark shapes flew through the mist over his head, and hundreds of wings blotted out the distant sun and cast threatening shadows on the flagstones below him.

His calls did not go unheard. A slew of soldiers poured out of the towers, flooding the battlements deserted only moments before. Valen watched in horror as the beasts lunged, bombing the first wave of recruits pointing their flaming arrows into the sky. Some managed to fire while others were taken away screaming into the mist.

It did not take long for chaos to erupt. Men ran back and forth, shooting arrows while stomping out flames, and others batted at the Elyndra's clutches. One man stumbled onto the prince, his face and body littered with bleeding scratches from the sharp claws. Valen helped him reach the lower deck and shouted for a healer. Once he knew the man was in good hands, Valen sprinted ahead, flaming sword in hand. Angered by the attacks on his fortress, he ripped through a mass of wings in a single arc.

He felled three Elyndra before claws wrapped around his body and he rose above the flagstones, feet unable to touch the ground. Valen flailed his arms and legs, twisting to stab it with his sword. Three flaps later, his head jerked up and down like a rag doll. Valen watched as the ground grew farther and farther away.

Suddenly, he heard a whizzing sound and then a crunching noise as someone's flaming arrow hit the beast's right wing. The Elyndra swayed in the air before dropping him. He felt a moment of numb weightlessness, and then his stomach pitched and he fell hard on the stone of the battlements.

After the initial shock had faded, Valen felt a flaring pain on his left side where he'd taken the brunt of the fall. Wincing, he rolled onto his other side and clutched the sore shoulder, feeling for broken bones. To his relief, every body part seemed to be in place. If anything, a dislocated shoulder was the least of his worries, and he still had his sword arm in working condition.

Valen swerved as he regained his footing and surveyed the upper battlements. The Elyndra clearly outnumbered Ravencliff's army. For each flying beast the soldiers brought down, two more sprang up. The continuous attacks were depleting the army.

As Valen reassessed the weakest point, he saw a sash of black and red through the crowd. "No. It can't be him." But another look in between searing arrows and sparkling wings revealed the king himself, lunging into battle as if he could do more good than sit on the throne.

"Father!" Valen shouted until his lungs threatened to burst, but no one could hear him over the ruckus of screams, clangs and the firing of cannons. He jumped past the archers sprawled underneath a cannon raised in the air and pushed through a congregation of healers waiting under the relative safety of the turrets. An entire battlefield sprawled between him and his father. Valen wove through the pandemonium, keeping the red-and-black target in sight. "Father!"

The king turned around, and for a brief heartbeat all Valen saw was rage in his father's eyes. Then his features softened as he focused on his son. Valen closed the distance between them just as another beast swooped above their heads. They both ducked and several archers fired. The beast fell behind them with arrows protruding from its body like a pin cushion.

"Father, what are you doing?"

"What I should have done a long time ago, son." The king's eyes held so much sadness it could engulf the world.

"What do you mean?"

"Helping this fortress. Putting duty ahead of my own personal agenda, even if it means that I have to kill every single one of them."

"But Father, there is no way you can defeat all them. You are just one man."

The king smiled. "I want to try."

Suddenly the sky darkened and both father and son looked up at the heavens. A new surge of beasts hovered over them, thick as a midnight quilt, flying wing to wing. It seemed as though the moment froze in time, a macabre pantomime, surreal in its clarity. For a moment, everyone stood still as if they all stared into their own deaths.

Then the fighting surged again in full force. Valen swung his sword with all his strength, his father at his back. It was the first time they'd been truly together in years, fighting at one another's side. Valen felt a rush of pride and sympathy for his estranged father, the one man who knew him so well yet stayed so far away. He wished he'd pressed their connection, gone and visited him in the long hours when the man closed himself off in the darkness of the throne room to drink and brood the night away.

His father was an impressive man, big and burly with arms the size of a horse's hind leg and a chest that rose round and firm above other's heads. He took down several beasts with one swing and little effort. Valen caught a glimpse of the king that had ridden into battle and charmed the hearts of the Ravencliff townspeople before he had a son.

The battle reached a lull and the endless tide of beasts dwindled. The soldiers cheered, thrusting their swords in the air as others lugged strewn sandbags to rebuild the wall. Valen's father appeared like a great war hero on the highest parapet, his cape fluttering in the wind. The crowd roared at his feet, chanting the king's name.

His father held up both hands and Valen saw a rare glimmer of happiness shine in his eyes. For a moment, Valen felt that everything would turn out all right and he'd have his father back the way he was before the accident. Wrapped up in the moment, Valen hollered with his fellow soldiers.

Just as the crowd's roar died down to hear his father speak, a great Elyndra, larger than the others, rose up from the mist beyond the wall and dove at the king. Valen watched as his father thrust his sword at its carapace. The beast spiraled in the air, avoiding the lunge and circled around for another plunge. The king gripped his sword with both hands and braced himself for another attack.

"Someone help him!" a soldier called out from the battlements, but Valen knew the king was too far up the parapet for anyone to reach him before the next attack. He stood in mute shock as the Elyndra swooped down, its massive wings batting the air.

The king lunged into the assault and his sword stuck in the beast's belly, but the force of its dive knocked him to the ground. The beast writhed on top of the king, who struggled to avoid its sharp talons.

"Father!" Valen leaped three steps at a time to the parapet. When he surfaced, the beast lay on his father, unmoving.

Valen grabbed one of the Elyndra's spindly legs and heaved the insect-like body off of his father, who lay on his back. The king dropped his sword and it clanged with finality on the stone. Valen crouched beside him. He could see a deep red blossoming out from underneath the red-and-black tunic, and he knew that a sharp talon had met its mark in the king's chest.

"Father." Valen watched as the older man's breathing grew more labored. He grabbed a soldier by the arm, jerking him away from his duties. "Find a healer! The king is down."

The soldier's eyes widened as he saw his king lying at his feet. "Yes, sir." He ran, signaling to other soldiers, and Valen knew the healers would come.

Valen looked into his father's eyes. "Don't worry, I've sent for help. You'll be all right." He felt as though he uttered a slim hope and nothing else.

The king coughed up droplets of red. The wound must have run deep because blood seeped out onto his belly. "Son, now you will be king."

"Don't talk like that. You will live."

But it seemed his father was not in the mood for daydreams. "Tell Bellanina that I love her, and give her mother my love also."

Valen felt his eyes filling with tears. "I will, but they know you love them."

His father rose out of his position to meet Valen eye to eye. Valen pressed him back down but could not keep him from speaking. "But you do not."

"That's not true, Father. I've known all along that you love me."

"The most." His father's gaze wandered. "The most of all."

"Father." Valen shook him, bringing him back to the present. He could no longer hold back his tears. They fell like raindrops on his father's bloodstained clothes.

"Valen, you must promise me something."

"Anything, Father, anything you ask."

"Promise me you will not make the same mistakes I did." His father took one last breath. "Promise me you will be a good king."

Valen swallowed hard. That was the one request he did not expect. It was not an easy task asked of him, but he knew the correct path to take and what he would have to give up.

His father's eyes grew blank and resolution took hold of Valen, a strong force that came from within. He brought his face close enough to lay a kiss on the man's cheek. "I promise."

Chapter 21

The Forgotten Ones

When Star emerged from the cave, she could see Leer's torch shining through the mist as he rode toward the sea of cocoons. He had a significant head start on her and she knew in the bottom of her churning stomach there was no way she could catch up.

Cursing under her breath, she kicked her heels into Windracer's sides, spurring the horse into action. Every hoofbeat down the slope, the fire spread like a rampant disease and the valley glowed with orange light. Leer had reached the bottom and spread ripples of flame throughout the mass of sleeping Elyndra. As she rode closer, she could see the men in brown robes race forward to stop him, leaving their posts vacant to save the burning cocoons.

Leer had been right. The havoc he created cleared a path to the machine. Star searched for him in the burning inferno raging below her but black smoke blinded her. She caught a glimpse of angry flames and thousands of black legs writhing like condemned souls in the broken sacks. She needed to get closer to yell his name, but there was no way down without injuring Windracer in the process. If she went after him, Star would put everything Leer had risked his life for in vain. He'd sealed the deal. The only task left to her was destroying the machine.

Waving smoke out of her eyes, Star spied a raised incline leading to the machine. She directed Windracer back around, out of the flames to the back of the canyon, and rode to meet her destiny. The hulk of metal rose before her, blotting out the sky until only oily black rose above her for miles.

The front was a never-ending slab of steel jutting out from the rock floor of the canyon. The machine looked like it fell on top of the earth eons ago and crushed an imprint in the sand. Although Star knew such a feat was impossible by any known means, she wouldn't put it past these people to figure out a way to build such a thing in the sky and land it on the ground. They'd already created a machine to help a species bent on death. More importantly, she had to find the way in.

Tying Windracer to an outcropping, Star examined the greasy front. She ran the palms of her hands back and forth across the moist substance congealing at the base, but could find no cracks or doorways of any kind. A rush of anxious nervousness threatened to overwhelm her. How could she follow through if she didn't even understand how to get in? How could she bring down such a mammoth of a beast? All at once, the task seemed daunting, and even more so because Leer had believed in her to the extent of sacrificing his own life. Now she stared blindly at her target, her voice mute and her weapons useless.

Star heard a strange, keen noise, like the call of a bird. Ten feet down the surface of the machine, the metal disappeared and a robed man came out. Distracted by the raging fire, he didn't even notice her as he ran toward the inferno below.

She watched as the man turned away, and then approached the hole where he'd come from. It had not been there seconds before. The metal surface had disappeared to reveal a long hallway, lit by strange green glowing globes with no fire in them. Star took one look back to make sure Windracer was safe then stepped inside. The structure hummed around her, as if it was a tuning fork struck centuries ago, still resounding. She followed the chain of globes magically illuminating the path in front of her. Metal surrounded her on all sides. The walls were cool and smooth to her touch, the surface slick and polished. If she looked closely, she could see her blurred reflection in the walls.

But Star had no time for examination. She had one purpose and one purpose alone. The heart of the beast should dwell deep inside, and so she used her well developed sense of direction and followed the humming, traveling ever farther into the core. Star passed boxes of flashing lights, magical panels of jeweled buttons and tubes winding around the walls like snakes. Making sure not to touch anything, she turned corner after corner, entering room after room of oddities. She felt trapped in someone else's strange dream.

As she journeyed through the belly of the machine, Star passed a long hallway lined with glass on all sides. She looked down to the level below. A laboratory with large translucent vials lined the walls. Elyndra, each in different stages of life, floated in the liquid substance in each tube. She could even see an embryo magnified by the thick walls of glass, the beginnings of a slender body and a slew of tangled legs. Then, a larva, small enough to hold in her hands, its skin white as ivory and delicate as silk. She gasped when she saw a giant caterpillar akin to the beasts from the forest, suspended in the gelatinous liquid, its groping mouth hanging open. Next came the lining of a cocoon, the beast inside taken out long ago. The body of an Elyndra in adult form hung from the ceiling, preserved by mist blowing through a vent in the wall. On the tables below were small dishes holding tiny white eggs the size of pearls, row upon row, glowing underneath the fluorescent globes, awaiting a new life.

Star's stomach heaved as she realized these people grew the Elyndra, harvested them and set them free upon the world. It was a twisted, symbiotic relationship she couldn't comprehend. All she knew was these robed men were her enemies and she had to stop them before another wave of flying beasts was unleashed to spread terror on Evenspark and Ravencliff.

Picking up her pace, Star jogged through the inner levels of the machine. Each hallway ran in a box-like shape around a centerpiece, with staircases at even intervals, taking the traveler to the next level. With each level, the turns in the hallways grew closer together, so that the new level surrounded the inner centerpiece, bringing her closer to the middle of the machine.

As the humming rose to a buzzing drawl pulsing in her inner ears, Star emerged from another long hallway into a room vast as a city square with rows and rows of tables arranged in concentric circles around a glowing sphere, which hovered above the floor, rotating like a small planet with sparks of iridescence and glimmering ribbons of light. It felt charged with energy and on the brink of instability, being contained only by some invisible force. A robed man stood in front of it, recording calculations on a raised table between him and the sphere.

Ducking underneath a table, Star watched the man for several moments. This orb must be the heart of the machine, the source of all its power. She watched as the man pressed buttons on the control panel in front of him, but could deduce no pattern to his motions or answer for how the sphere stayed in equilateral suspension.

He murmured a strange litany of numbers and names into a black grid-like film in the console. "The tenth of November, 4671 AD, at five twenty-seven." Star thought about his words but no meaning came to mind.

After several moments of pressing seemingly random buttons, the man poured a thick liquid substance into a tube running from the console to the orb. Star wondered if the tube was the weakest spot, the one way to get past the force field surrounding the energy ball.

Star's fingers shook and she felt as though all the nervous bubbles running through her system would explode all at once. She knew her time was running out. Leer could not keep all of the robed men away forever. She had to make her move.

She crept toward the man at the front table, sliding her dagger out of its sheath in her boot and calculating her moves. Just as the man bent to pick up a strange writing utensil from the floor, Star leaped, knocking him on the ground. Before he could react, she had her dagger glinting at his throat.

The man stared, dazed and confused before fear entered its way into his eyes, which grew wide, as if he looked on a ghost.

Star noticed the clasp on his robe, the same symbol she'd seen on the assassination letter addressed to Leer. She'd always thought the man in the insignia had slain the Elyndra, but now she knew the pewter figure engraved on the symbol reached toward the beast to honor it.

The man snatched the clasp away from her. "You've come to destroy us all."

Star's anger raged. "I've come to put a stop to this madness."

"You've brought the madness with you."

She was in no mood to argue as she pressed the dagger against the heated skin of his neck. "I need to know how to stop the machine. Tell me now and you will live."

The man did not speak. Why would he give up all their answers now? She contemplated what to do with him as he looked at her in terror. If any of his friends showed up, perhaps she could use him as a hostage, even negotiate him for Leer if he had managed to survive and they captured him.

"Fine." She brought out a rope from her pocket and tied his hands behind his back. She bound another rope tightly around his feet. Once Star secured him, she walked toward the console, looking over the alien symbols and flashing lights. She watched his face carefully as her hand passed over certain controls. But he did not move. His fear vanished as he smiled in bliss.

"There is no way, with your primitive intelligence, to figure it out."

Star felt the stab but did not let it show on her features. She knew she was in over her head, and more brown-robed help would be coming soon.

So she pushed buttons, all the buttons. There were some flashes, a few beeps and then nothing. To her chagrin, the man tied on the floor sat back with relief.

Then her fingers brushed the tube. Attached to the console by a clamp, it shot out into the glowing globe like an umbilical cord. Star wondered if she had anything small enough to put in it and sharp enough to cause a tear or an obstruction. She thought about coins, and rummaged through her pockets, but as ever, she was penniless. She thought about matches, and set one aflame, but the fire sizzled out in the gel-like liquid on the way down. In the background, the robed man laughed, enjoying some secret joke.

Star remembered the necklace Valen had given her as a present for saving Bellanina's bunnyfly. She'd worn it every day since, the chain clasped around her neck and the ruby heart hidden beneath the folds of her traveling tunic. It was the perfect size to clog the tube. Unclasping the necklace from around her neck, she pulled it out from underneath her layers of clothing and held it above the tube in a moment of indecision. It glowed faintly red throughout the chamber.

"Wait!" The man's expression turned into fear. "Don't drop that in! You'll ruin everything!"

Star whirled around, her trance with the necklace broken. Somehow she'd struck the right chord.

"If you drop the jewel in, we will all suffer. The planet will die."

The pendant hung above the rim, swinging back and forth like a pendulum. Star shot a glance back at him. "What do you mean?"

"This machine controls the equilibrium of life on this world. Without it, chaos will reign unchallenged."

"It seems to me all the machine controls is that awful mist."

"Which is the life force of all the Elyndra."

"Then they should all die." The pendant dropped a bit farther.

"No," the man pleaded, his voice hoarse. "You don't understand."

"You've got one minute to explain."

The man sighed like she'd asked an impossible task. He shifted on the floor and straightened his back, as if to gain force with his voice and collect his thoughts. "Ages ago, our ancestors were forced to leave their home world. There was no balance, no one to oversee the population, and the world grew full with people and nothing else. All other species became extinct. Resources dwindled. They sent out ships to colonize other worlds, but the pattern kept repeating on and on again.

"Our ancestors, The Forgotten Ones, were like a virus, spreading death on each consecutive planet they reached. It took generations upon generations, but the end was always the same, until our ancestors devised a solution. They chose this planet with a purpose, to coexist. Don't you see? The Elyndra are the check in the system, the solution to the problem. If we kill them, then we kill this world."

Star's eyes flared as if she talked to a child who didn't want to listen. "The mist has taken over. It's invaded our territories. The Elyndra will kill us all."

The man shook his head, bitterness simmering in his eyes. "It is you that have taken over, your cities sprawling out onto preserved land. Without the mist, what is there to stop you from taking over the entire planet?"

The sheer thought of other worlds bent Star's mind, never mind the concept of lands full of people and nothing else. Between Ravencliff and Evenspark alone, there was enough room for hundreds of new towns and thousands more people. "The Elyndra are attacking my friends. If I don't stop them, the people, my family, will die."

The man's shoulders drooped. "Then you doom us all."

Star hovered on the brink of a great and everlasting decision. She knew that what he spoke was beyond her comprehension and she was not a god with license to choose the fate of an entire world. But then she thought of Leer, how he'd been so eager to fight for her cause, of her parents in their wispy home on the outskirts and of Valen watching the walls of Ravencliff each day. She could not let them down.

She was not the one to make such a monumental decision about life and fate, but neither was this cold-hearted, monster-breeding scientist boasting all the knowledge in the universe but knowing nothing of family, of love.

Star dropped the necklace and it fell into the depths of the tube. She watched in silent horror and awe as it traveled up to the orb, pulsing red in the glowing light. The robed man shouted and sobbed behind her, praying, but the necklace moved steadfastly, right to the sphere's inner core.

Chapter 22

King

"They've breached the walls, Your Highness. We must fall back!"

Valen slashed through the air, his sword finding another flying target. Although they'd achieved a lull in the fighting, the numbers of Elyndra rose again in the last few hours, dozens of them flinging themselves at Ravencliff's walls. He feared some had even managed to get through their barricade and now wreaked havoc on the streets below. He hoped soldiers and pedestrians alike had heeded his bugle call and were fortified inside their homes.

"If we retreat now, there is no turning back!" Valen gritted his teeth. Sweat and blood wet his tunic, and his arms and legs hurt like he'd been torn apart by racing stallions. But he was not yet ready to give up.

"Your Highness," the man said, bowing in all humbleness, "the troops are dying. If we don't fall back now, no one will be left."

Valen stared the man down, his face inches away. "Do you want to live in a hole in the ground for the rest of your life? To never see the light of day?"

The man nodded. "I want to live."

Just then, an Elyndra crashed into what was left of the sand bags stacked on the barricade. Grit spewed around them, raining on their heads. Then the wall of mist poured in.

Valen turned and shouted across the battlements, "Fall back!" Other soldiers echoed his cry, eager to be behind a stone wall and under a roof.

"Go on." Valen looked at the man, wondering why he remained. "Get everyone inside." Valen saw the man's uniform, trying to determine his rank, and realized this was not a soldier from his army at all. Underneath the blue velvet overcoat was a white shirt and overalls. He was a villager who wore a lowly officer's coat and had come to fight.

"What about you, Your Highness?"

Valen wondered if he should say anything about the man's station and decided against it. If he wanted to fight, then so be it. They needed all the men they could get.

The man stood in front of him, awaiting his answer. Valen wiped sweat from his forehead. "I'm not going in until everyone out here is safely behind those walls."

But the counterfeit soldier refused to leave. He stepped toward Valen, blocking his path. "Sir, you must be protected. You must be the first to go back."

"That's the damndest thing I've ever heard. I have to man these battlements." Valen pushed forward but the man grabbed his arm.

"No, Your Highness. We need you alive. We need a leader."

Valen froze in place with the man's words. His father had died only a few moments ago and it hadn't sunk in he was their new king. In fact, if something happened to him, the next in line would be Bellanina, and she wasn't even old enough to lace her own slippers. He might as well put her bunnyfly in charge. Ducking under the overhang of the turret, Valen realized just how important his decisions and actions were.

"You're right." He stumbled back, his hurt arm falling to dangle limply at his side as the battle stress caught up to him and weariness set in.

The man supported his weight. "I'll see to it all remaining soldiers get inside."

Before Valen could react, two passing healers ushered him down the twirling stone staircase leading from the turret to the inner battlements. As he looked back, he saw the velvet-coated back of the fake soldier as he entered the cloud of mist.

* * * *

"What do we do? Run across the courtyard, out in the open?" The healer turned to Valen with eyes wild with fear. They'd reached the bottom of the turret. The mist had seeped over the fortress walls and was flooding the main square. A hundred meters separated them from the fortified training hall.

Valen peered out into the mist, seeing only vague shadows. "We have to. We can't stay here. There isn't any food or water, and we don't know how long we'll be trapped."

The healer was reluctant to go. "Can't we wait until help gets here?"

"We are the help." Valen put a hand on her shoulder and surveyed the ragtag group following him. "What's left of it, anyway."

He wondered how many Elyndra had managed to get past the remaining soldiers on the walls. If any had made it through, the soldiers would be picked off like deer in an open field. He didn't think the healers or the wounded would be able to outrun them.

Valen shouted to the crowd flooding the stairway, "Are there any archers left?"

"Yes, sir." Valen recognized the young man as John Hall, barely graduated from the academy.

"Will you cover us as we run across?"

The young man nodded and pulled an arrow from the quiver on his back. "I'll do the best I can."

"Good." Valen tried to summon a reassuring smile. "Once we're out of sight, run like Hell's on your heels, you hear me?"

John nodded, taking position in the doorway. "I will, Your Highness."

"Come on." Valen took the old healer's arm. "Let's go."

Running through the mist was like a strange, ethereal dream, the courtyard turning into an otherworldly cloud city. It was eerie and calm, unlike the chaos raging behind them on the crumbling walls.

"Stay together," Valen ordered between heaves of air. He dragged both old women forward as they huddled under their healers' shawls, half-paralyzed by fear. Behind him, he could hear faint shifts of wind as John fired shafts of arrows through the air.

A man screamed to his right, and Valen whirled around in time to see him plucked from the flagstone, his legs dangling in the air, grasping for the ground. Another solider went to help, but Valen held him back. "It's useless. We have to keep going." The healer on his left arm sobbed, but Valen pulled her along.

The remaining survivors retreated in a cluster. Up above, they could still hear John's arrows as they found their targets. Valen was thankful the archer had a good eye and aim.

When they reached the supply hall, it was empty. Valen ushered the soldiers in as fast as he could, watching the sky above. He waited for John, leaving the door open halfway and praying the young lad had managed to run behind them. In a few moments, the archer appeared out of nowhere, spooking Valen for a split second as he threw his body against the door.

"Well done, John." Valen patted him gently on the back.

The archer shook his head, steadying himself and gasping for air. "That was close."

"It's because of you we are all here alive."

John waved him away with his bow. "Nonsense. It's because of you, Your Highness, that we've made it this far."

Valen felt a pang of gratitude. His eyes brimmed with tears, but he held them back. There was no time for emotional exchanges.

After he secured the door behind him, Valen turned and surveyed the room. There were a dozen soldiers, all in varying conditions, and two healers—the remnants of Ravencliff's great and illustrious army. He hoped the others had made it off the battlements and found an alternate hiding place.

He was glad to see Allyn there. Although he was uninjured, dark circles framed his eyes. Valen remembered with a sharp pang the young man's father was also gone.

Suppressing a wave of grief, Valen looked at the men with the least serious wounds. "Help me board the windows. Put anything you can in their way, but leave a hole big enough for us to see out. John, keep watch outside. If anyone is alive out there, cover them as they find shelter."

"Yes, sir."

Valen saw the stronger of the two healers rummaging around. She counted the cans and bottles, making lists. "How many supplies do we have?" He eyed the small cupboards. This was a weapons depot. It was not used for the storage of food or water. What was left were the soldier's packed lunches, a few bags of rice and a pitcher of ale.

The old woman's lips quivered. "With fifteen people, two days, at most."

"Ration the food." Valen pointed toward a table at the far end. "Give priority to the weak and wounded."

"Yes, Your Highness." The healer bowed her head and collected the supplies. Valen hoped his instructions gave her strength. He could use some strength himself. Their fate rested in his hands now.

Valen picked his way through the throng of wounded soldiers to gaze through the small hole in the boards. Mist drowned the courtyard and he felt as though his castle had been dropped into another land.

"What will we do, Your Highness?" John clutched his quiver. Less than a dozen arrows were left. He found a crude knife and began sharpening the end of a few scraps of wood for makeshift arrows.

"Wait." Valen thought of Star, riding her midnight horse through the countryside, her white hair shining behind her like a celestial flag. "There is still hope left."

Chapter 23

Identification Tags

The ruby pendant disappeared into the sphere. Nothing happened and Star lowered her shoulders in defeat. The sphere likely disintegrated the ruby before it could cause a disturbance in the field. She turned to the Forgotten One, expecting to see an expression of relief, but his features were tinged with fear. He stared at the globe as if it would explode right there and kill them both.

A crackling sound tickled her ears and she smelled sulfurous smoke. Star whirled back around and saw dark, tiny bursts peppering the sphere's surface, like sun spots. The dark blobs spread as fast as spilled ink, spiraling out in ebony ripples in dark, ominous tides. Tiny explosions disturbed the surface, sending sparks flying through the air like falling stars. The humming pulsated now, becoming louder with each sound wave.

She ducked and shielded her face with her arm. It didn't take a scientist to know the sphere had lost its equilibrium and could not be contained. Soon the pressure would force it to burst.

She unsheathed her dagger and cut the rope holding the man's heels together. "Go on! Get out of here."

The man refused to move. She pulled him up, but his limbs fell limp. "It doesn't matter now. All is lost. Everything I've ever worked for is done."

Star shook his arm. "Why can't our people be different? Why can't we change our fate?"

The man shook his head slowly, as if he knew so much and she, so little. "You are just like all the rest of them, don't you see? Too nice to set rules on life." He looked as if he'd told her she had some grotesque disease. "Your heart is too big."

Tears streaked Star's face. "I don't understand what you mean."

The man closed his eyes. "William Wordsworth had it right, two thousand and eight hundred years back in 1802." He then recited lines, as if he chanted a spell that would undo all that Star had done.

> *The world is too much with us, late and soon,*
> *Getting and spending, we lay waste our*
> *powers.*
> *Little we see in Nature that is ours,*
> *We have given our hearts away, a sordid boon!*
> *This Sea that bares her bosom to the moon,*
> *The winds that will be howling at all hours,*
> *And are up-gathered now like sleeping flowers,*
> *For this, for everything, we are out of tune.*

Star took his arm and tried to drag him up, but a large spark from the sphere barreled toward them, landing on the console like a meteor and setting all the wires aflame. The force of the explosion threw Star backward underneath the tables. She landed several feet away. Rubbing her bruised elbow, she heard the man scream and looked up with horror. The orb grew larger with each second. It had engulfed the area around it with its spinning particles, absorbing the console.

The man shouted, "Now only you know the truth!" As he spoke, he vanished into the orb's light as if he'd never existed at all.

Star pulled herself out from under the table and scrambled to her feet. Without looking back, she threw herself into the hallway and stumbled down the metal corridor, falling each time another explosion hit. The air behind her grew so hot she thought her hair would burn. Smoke poured around her and she had to feel her way down the first stairwell, coughing until her lungs ached.

It seemed like she would never outrun the explosion. Cables and hoses fell from the ceiling, tangling her arms and legs as she ran. Steam blew in hot bursts of air over her head, the pipes exploding under the pressure. Somewhere behind her, she heard a man scream.

She descended level after level of burning inferno. She counted her steps, two at a time, trying to make sense of the structure and ensure she headed toward the exit.

Another explosion hit and Star tumbled onto the floor. The machine retched like an earthquake rumbled underneath it. A puff of smoke filled the air. Star coughed and wheezed, spitting ash. Dizziness threatened to overtake her and she forced herself to breath deeply until she could regain a measure of control.

When the air cleared, she opened her eyes and screamed. A man lay on the floor beside her, the back of his head crushed by a fallen panel from the ceiling. Star looked into his vacant eyes, noticed his freshly shaven skin, and watched as the blood trickled down across his forehead, funneling around his ear. Underneath his chin was the same clasp on his robe with the pewter engraving of the man with the beast. Star took the metal inscription in her hand and ripped it from his robe in one clean yank. She would need it for proof when she got back.

If she got back.

A rumbling tremor threatened another seismic quake. Star picked herself up, dropped the clasp into her pocket and continued her sprint to safety. The air felt cooler as she ran and she knew she was close to the outside. A fresh breeze flooded in, and she turned the corner and saw the hallway where she came in, the door carelessly left open. Star felt a pang of guilt for leaving Windracer out there and silently prayed her horse was safe.

She stopped at the threshold of the machine. Fires raged below her in all directions and she felt as though she stood witness to the end of the world. She looked for Leer but her eyes played tricks on her. In one instant, she saw the burning outline of a horse. The next it was just flames, all-consuming, with nothing left.

She heard Windracer's whinny and saw the black horse pulling back on the reins tying her to the rock wall. The fires spread and soon she would also be in danger. Star ran across the front of the machine to Windracer. "We're going to be all right!"

Star untied the reins and jumped on Windracer's back. There was no way down to the cocoons, and no way to tell if Leer had made it. Smoke and flame filled the entire gorge and the machine would soon blow. She had to get out of the canyon before it exploded. There was nowhere else to go.

Sniffing back tears, Star kicked Windracer's sides and they took off up the ledge. She kept looking over her shoulder only to see sparks fly through the haze as the machine gave its final chug of mist. As she ascended the path up to the ledge, Star stopped at the cavern where she and Leer had stayed the previous night, holding on to the distant hope he'd made it and was waiting for her.

Windracer offered a snort of protest, but Star led her up the ledge despite the raging fire growing below and the time bomb ticking at the canyon's center. She passed the place where Leer had kissed her, and then the inner cavern where they'd made camp. The floor was still littered with their footprints, their sleeping bags placed side by side.

The cavern was empty. And she had just wasted more precious seconds.

Star looked at the opposite wall and stifled a sob. Leer had left his tags hanging on an outcropping, as if he already knew he wouldn't live. She dismounted and ran over. Star took the tags in her palm, the metal chiming. She smoothed her fingertips over the indentations etched in silver. The numbers seemed random, but to her they held all the significance in the world. In a rash decision, she put the chain around her own neck, the tags resting between her breasts where Valen's ruby heart once nestled.

Wiping away fresh tears, Star led Windracer back to the canyon's ledge. The smoke had surpassed them when they were in the cave, and she couldn't see anything beyond the extension of her forearm. With a rush of panic, Star jumped back on Windracer and they hurried up the steep cliff face as fast as they could without losing balance or footing. A chain of explosions shattered her eardrums and she knew the machine's orb had pulsed its last throb, taking everything in the canyon along with it. Tears streaked her ash-stained face. She felt as though she'd left a part of her heart behind.

Star reached the top of the canyon and paused, looking down into the havoc she'd help create. Flames the size of buildings licked the air, and the smoke rose in a haystack tunnel, polluting the horizon for miles before it tapered away beyond the clouds. She was certain all the Elyndra were burnt to cinders, their fragile wings incinerated instantly. They no longer threatened the air above her head.

Star searched the rim of the canyon for the rest of the day and into the night, calling out Leer's name. To her horror, she could find no other way down, which meant there was no alternate exit. Consumed with an immense sense of loss, it took Star long moments before she accepted the fact she would not find him that day and settled into a makeshift camp. Only after she released her grief, the feelings washing over her in tidal waves, that she noticed the mist was gone.

Chapter 24

Savior

Valen broke the last crust of stale bread in his hands, breaking it into fourteen even pieces. Holding back tears, he walked around the room, handing the crumbs to each survivor as if it was their last meal.

"What about you, Your Highness?" John pushed his own ration away. "You haven't eaten in days."

"I'll eat when those blasted beasts are dead and gone." Valen looked back at John, who kept watch by the boarded window. "You'll need nourishment if you want to keep your aim sharp."

John sighed. "What does it matter? We're stuck here like rats in a cage."

Valen leaned forward, drawing near to whisper in his ear. "I mean to make a run for it. Take our best fighters and, under your cover, run to the nearest shop to retrieve more food for the others."

John looked horrified. "That's suicide. You'll never make it there, never mind make it back again."

"We have to do something. We're out of supplies."

"They know that we're in here. Those beasts are not dumb. They're biding their time, waiting patiently for one of us to come out. I won't let you kill yourself. You are the king and we need your leadership."

"What we need is food." Valen turned to the others huddling against each other in the shadows of the supply hall. They dared not light anything more than a single candle for fear any light or warmth would attract the beasts. There were too many out there to kill with the amount of flames they could produce.

"I'm going out in search of more food and supplies. I will go by myself if I have to, but I'm looking for volunteers to run with me."

Valen watched as the soldiers looked from him to one another, weighing in the possibilities and likelihood they could make it there and back unharmed. Although higher numbers would secure a better chance of transporting food, he didn't want to pressure anyone to make a decision concerning life or death. It was their choice and theirs alone.

"I'll go." Allyn held up his sword. Sadness hit Valen at the sight of this young man's bravery in the absence of his father. Commander Rile would be proud of his son.

"Count me in." John clapped Allyn on the back. "Like I said, I won't let you kill yourself. If it's up to me, King Valen, then you'll be well protected."

Valen felt a bolt of shock with the word *king*. He felt as if they handed him a sword too big to wield. Looking at the fear and hope in each soldier's face made him straighten up and realize that he was all they had. Silently he promised them he would be the best ruler he could be.

One soldier after another got up slowly from the makeshift bedding on the floor, dusting off their armor to be used once again. Valen watched and nodded to each solider in turn. A sense of camaraderie washed over him along with an overwhelming feeling of the vast responsibility set upon his shoulders. They were his subjects now, and they put their faith in his tactics and depended on his decisions as king. He only hoped he didn't lead them all to their untimely deaths.

In all, Valen chose only two soldiers to go with him. The remaining volunteers were too old, too burly or too injured to be able to run fast enough, hide underneath wagons and dodge the incoming attacks. Valen would lead the way, followed by Allyn and John in the rear. Valen's strength lay in his sword, Allyn was agile, and John had excellent aim. He could cover them the entire way, following a step behind to watch over their heads.

"Close the door behind us," Valen said to the healer who huddled underneath her robes. "If all goes as planned, we'll be back before nightfall with food and supplies."

Silence fell as Valen opened the main door. The mist flowed in an ominous tide, insidious tendrils unfurling to caress the stockroom floor. John cocked an arrow, pointing into the sky. A brief movement fluttered overhead then all was silent. Valen couldn't tell if it was a trap.

"Come on." Valen waved to Allyn and dashed into the mist. The young man held his breath and went after him. Grasping his bow, John followed, close behind.

Valen heard the door shut tightly as he veered in and out of the debris on the street, searching for the next place to hide. There were overturned wagons, bags of merchandise littering the cobblestone and, worst of all, blood stains. Valen felt like a wandering spirit in an ethereal ghost town. Being out in the open felt strange after having huddled in the dark for two days.

They ran fifty paces before he felt a swish over his head and ducked, somersaulting onto his back. "Watch out! They know we're here."

He heard another arrow fly as John fought them off. Valen jumped into an abandoned carriage and put out his hand for Allyn. The young man reached out and allowed himself to be pulled up, but Valen refused to close the door.

"John!" he yelled into the misty void. "We're over here."

John released two more arrows and made his way to the carriage. Valen hefted him up and they closed the door behind them, peering out the glass panel like weary travelers on the road to the underworld.

Suddenly an Elyndra landed on the carriage top, sending the entire box shaking. Valen was relieved this particular carriage was an upscale model, with a roof of wood instead of linen. There was no way it could get through.

"Don't move." Valen held up a hand in warning. "It may not have seen us go in. In fact, it's probably just probing around."

John held his bow against his chest and closed his eyes. Allyn kept his face glued to the glass, breath fogging on the pane. Valen could see nothing through the mist, but if it made Allyn feel better to watch, then so be it. Valen felt safe as long as none of them moved.

A few minutes later, the Elyndra took off, shaking the carriage once again.

"Do you think it's safe to go outside?" Allyn's hand rested on the door lock.

Valen didn't want to keep the hungry soldiers waiting any longer, but if anything happened to them, they'd be waiting forever. "What do you think, John?"

The archer shrugged. "What's fifteen more minutes going to do?"

Valen placed a hand on Allyn's shoulder. "For now we wait."

He searched the carriage for anything that might help them. A pair of discarded velvet gloves, an embroidered cushion and a crushed sunhat lay scattered on the floor. It wasn't like the citizens carried extravagant weapons with them through the city. Their suitcases would be fastened to the top, but most likely they would be packed with clothes and toiletries.

Valen sat back in the velvet-cushioned seat, Allyn on one side and John on the other. In any other circumstance, it would be quite hilarious—a prince cum king, an archer and a foot soldier, riding together in finery.

Several moments later, Valen chanced opening the carriage door. Allyn cringed as Valen threw out the sunhat as bait. They watched and waited, but nothing descended to investigate.

Valen released a long breath of relief. "Our best bet is to run down Ravennest Alley, right to Harry's General Shop. That's the closest store I can think of."

John nodded. "Hopefully he'll have a sale on arrows."

Allyn's eyes widened. "How many do you have left?"

"Including this one, five."

"Don't worry." Valen winked at Allyn. "That's enough to cover us. John is an excellent shot."

"I certainly hope so," the young man replied.

Valen jumped to the ground. After taking a few hesitant steps, he signaled for Allyn and John to follow. "Stay close behind me." He turned and disappeared into the wall of mist.

Ravennest Alley had a series of overhangings meant to keep the citizens protected from the rain. The trio ran underneath them, shuffling past breaks in the awnings as fast as they could.

When they got to the store, the front door was locked.

"Damn it!" Valen pounded his fist on the thick wood. "Let us in!"

But the store was a large room, and Harry himself lived upstairs. If he was in the backroom hiding from the apparent apocalypse, there was no way of getting his attention.

The awnings behind them moved in an unnatural breeze and Valen knew the beasts had tracked them.

"What do we do?" Panic edged Allyn's voice.

John cocked an arrow in the direction of the movement. "Just keep pounding on the door."

Valen smacked the wood desperately, but it would not budge. Harry had probably boarded all the openings by now. "It's useless."

Allyn's gaze kept darting up to the awnings fluttering above their heads. "Can we find another place to hide?"

Valen scoured the alley, but the street was empty. There weren't even any barrels or stalls set up for passersby. In resignation, he took out his sword. He looked at the fallen commander's son with pity. He was so young and so brave. "Allyn, you're going to have to fight."

A rush of wind distracted Valen, blowing his hair out of his eyes. The mist swirled and blew past them, and they heard large thumps as the beasts hit the ground. Valen thought the Elyndra would all die right then, that they landed to battle them head to head.

Then the white wisps flowed around them and cleared. The mist had run out.

"What's going on?" Allyn squinted against the cold northern wind.

"The Elyndra." John lowered his bow in shock. "They are dying."

Before Valen could warn him, Allyn ran back down the alley. Valen ran after him, followed by John. When they caught up, the young man kicked an Elyndra in the left wing as it disintegrated in the dry air.

"Would you look at that!" Allyn's laughter bordered on hysteria. "We are saved."

John crouched beside the exoskeleton. He pulled on a talon and the entire leg crumbled to the ground in dust. "But how can this be? For as long as we ever lived, the mist has only grown stronger. It never relented."

"Star." Valen's chest burned with pride. "She made it. She's saved us all."

Chapter 25

Hero's Return

Star rode through a graveyard littered with winged exoskeletons. To either side of her lay a vast expanse of open land. The mountains that had harbored her and Leer on their journey there protruded on the horizon to the west, and in front of her sprawled the dark forest. Direction was no longer an issue. She had a clear sight of her path. Although it made for easier riding, Star craved the trees' dense canopy, feeling naked in the stark plains without the mist to cover her tracks.

She had to remind herself her instincts for cover were no longer necessary, there was no need to fear. The monsters were only a lingering memory. Their bodies lay dead before her like a garden of poisoned weeds. Windracer wove in and out of the fallen corpses as they plowed their way back to Ravencliff.

She'd stayed at the ravine's edge for three days and still the fires burned bright like the gates to Hell. Leer was nowhere to be found and her supplies diminished. She felt a growing need to return to Ravencliff, fearing all her efforts were too late. Leaving empty handed broke her heart and Star cried each minute Windracer took her away, but she had to move on in body if not in spirit.

Star reached the forest by nightfall and camped underneath the canopy. Her small fire was a faint radiance compared to the brightness of the full moon as it filtered through the leaves to touch the forest floor for the first time in ages. Star reached out to the diaphanous glow, her palm illuminated as she cradled the light. It seemed to shine only for her, a beacon from heaven to soothe a restless soul.

The giant caterpillars were gone. She wondered if they writhed on the heels of the last breath of mist, too slow to catch it as it abandoned the land like a defeated army. They, too, would drown in the dry air, dehydrated by parched wind as it burned and cracked their skin. Part of her felt sorry for the beasts that would never reach their full potential and fly in the sky, but a greater part of her finally felt safe for the first time in her life.

She broke through the forest the next day. Without the mist, the journey seemed effortless, the riding all too easy. She would be back at Ravencliff within the next day. Anxiety overshadowed her sadness as she remembered just how far the mist had risen and wondered if anyone was still alive within those walls. A thousand gruesome images plagued her imagination as she thought of all the possible scenes awaiting her when she returned.

Star got her answer miles before she reached Ravencliff's walls. Tiny dots moved on the horizon. As Windracer brought Star closer, she could make out people, without protection, roaming the countryside. The freedom brought more tears to her eyes. As she grew closer, she saw they were building, expanding Ravencliff's territories beyond the fortress.

Windracer picked up pace, riding in their direction, as if the horse were eager for the company of others. Star smoothed her horse's mane as if to say she felt the excitement as well.

The people walking the countryside hailed her as she pulled up, hands rising in the air in a universal gesture of peace. Star reined her horse in and slowed to a halt, drawing the attention of the new colonizers. One by one, they stopped their hammering and gathered together to meet the strange rider from the north. She thought she heard someone whisper *white rider* and wondered how she'd come to be so well known.

"You must be Star Nightengale." The closest man approached her as she dismounted. The others stared at her as if she were a demigod.

"I am." Star was baffled by their hushed awe and respect.

"The king has uttered your name as our savior, the white rider who rode to stop the mist. The one who saved us all."

"The king?" Star hadn't ever met the king. Valen must have told him of her quest.

"Oh, yes. He sent scouts to look for you when the mist ended. We feared you perished."

She looked down at the ground. "One of us did. He is the true hero."

The men fell silent around her, and she saw faces full of gratitude and hope.

Another man spoke. "He did not die in vain."

Star recognized the speaker right away. He was the fiddle player who had stood next to her in line when she returned the bunnyfly. She sniffed back tears. "So you've finally found a home, I take it."

The man bowed his head. "Thanks to you and the man who died, we all have."

"Leer." Star rubbed her sore eyes. "His name was Fallon Leer."

* * * *

The drawbridge to Ravencliff hung open like a shocked woman's mouth. Star rode past children as they ran through the meadows just outside of the walls. One little girl held a basket of dandelions and skipped alongside her to bring them home. She smiled shyly at Star as she rode past. All of the children waved, arms reaching above the wildflowers and long stems of grass.

Star dismounted and led Windracer inside the gate. Ravencliff's walls were not what she remembered. Large piles of black debris burned and smoked, tainting the air. Sections of the wall were missing and scars scratched the stone from stray swords and arrows. Weary guards hobbled and poked at the flames. The courtyard looked like it had been hit by an apocalypse. She could only imagine how terrible the battle could have been.

The same gruff soldier stood at the entranceway. This time, he let her by without question even though she no longer carried a sack of letters. "So you made it, huh?"

Star nodded. "Just barely."

"The king would like to see you, I'm sure." He handed her a pass to the castle at the center of the city.

"Tell me." Star stretched her neck, looking around her. "How many were lost in the battle while I was gone?"

The soldier leaned back and took in a deep breath. He adjusted his seat to favor his right side. Star could see his left leg underneath the table was bandaged from the knee down. "Most of the army. We are almost defenseless against Evenspark's troops. They could march in and take us over any day."

"And Prince Valen." Star's voice faltered. "Is he all right?"

"That's King Valen now, and His Highness is in good health, if not stressed from the efforts to rebuild."

"King." Star stumbled back against Windracer.

The guard went back to shuffling his papers. "That's right. Crowned yesterday."

Star carried the shock of the thought of Valen as king all the way to the palace steps. In a way, she was happy for him. He'd practically been acting as king for many years now and he deserved it. However, for her, it had happened too fast, too soon, and without her being there to accept his change in status. It seemed like she returned to a different world, an alternate reality of her own accidental creation.

An attendant ushered her down the main entrance hall, past corridors of closed doors and to the king's study, whispers of *savior* following behind her. Star felt uncomfortable with this newly found honor and shooed them back, only to have them bow and stare in awe.

She arrived at a rich mahogany door, and the attendant knocked the brass ring before she was ready. Star knew no matter how much time she had, she would never be truly ready to come face to face with Valen as king. The door opened and there he sat, perched behind his desk in a regal suit with medals of valor shining.

The attendant bowed. "Miss Star Nightengale, Your Highness."

Star could see a profound sadness in Valen's eyes that had not been there before, a weight on his shoulders holding him down. Beyond all that, she could sense his relief to see her.

"My goodness, I've had search parties scour the lands for you." He dismissed the other attendants in the room with a wave and he and Star waited in awkward silence until the last of them left. Star thought he would come over to her, yet he stayed on the other side of his desk, still as a statue. To her, it felt a world away.

"I stayed behind to look for Leer."

"He didn't abandon you, did he?"

Valen's distrust of his cousin hurt her. Her own words came out harsher than she meant. "How dare you question him! He died helping me in my quest."

Surprise flared on Valen's features, followed by melancholy and, underneath it all, pride. He looked away to a window facing north. Star could see an inner battle waging beneath his severely controlled features and tightened lips.

Star stepped forward. "He was not going to assassinate you. In fact, he was looking for their leader, looking to redeem himself and make things right again between the two of you."

"There was no need. I'd forgiven him long ago."

Although she'd only spent a few days with Leer, Star felt like she knew his mysterious ways better than anyone else in the world. He had opened up to her and showed her the shape of his heart. "It was important to him."

Valen placed his hand on his desk. "He will go down as a hero."

"He should." Star held his gaze. A threat edged her tone. "And no less."

"Of course." Valen looked away as if other thoughts preoccupied him.

"Leer and I found who ordered your assassination attempt." Star reached into her pocket and found the clasp with the symbol engraved. She threw it on the desk in front of him and it hit the expensive wood with a rude clang. "There are spies in our neighboring kingdoms, people who controlled the mist and the Elyndra. They said our population rose too high, expanding our boundaries, and they wanted war."

Star watched as Valen took the clasp in his hand. He brought out a piece of parchment, and she was surprised to see it was the assassination letter. She speculated if it was one of the heavy objects chaining him down.

"The symbol does match, yes." Valen paused. "How do we stop these people?"

"I already have. Their mist machine is destroyed and the Elyndra are dead. If any survivors exist, they have scattered. All you need to do is weed out the spies within your own walls. I will take care of their co-conspirators in Evenspark."

"I'll have my people get on it right away." Pain stretched in Valen's face. "You've done so much for this kingdom, for my people, and I am eternally in your debt." His eyelids grew heavy and dark. "I have one last favor to ask."

Star leaned forward. "Anything."

"Things have changed. Ravencliff is not the power it used to be. We've been decimated by the Elyndra. We have no army to protect us, no way to keep our borders. Without the mist, there is nothing holding Evenspark's army back."

"And you think Evenspark will attack?"

Valen's gaze was steady and intense. "I know it for certain."

Star studied the depth in his eyes and the lines etched in his face. Not only had he changed, but she'd changed as well. Somehow, the air between them had grown stale. He'd lost his youthful rebelliousness in the battle, and she'd lost her heart in the ruins of the canyon.

That didn't mean she didn't care. She'd spent so long saving the kingdom and didn't want to see them lose again. The Elyndra had spilled so much blood, it felt like there was none left to give. "What can I do to help?"

"You told me once, long ago, you make your own destiny."

His words tugged on her memories and her thoughts scrambled to a scene way back, when she'd met a young man at the fountain after she'd won the most important race of her life. She'd been daring and mischievous in the rush of youth and he'd been hesitant and questioning,

Aubrie Dionne

still exploring new ideals. "I remember now. You told me that fate rewarded me."

The corners of Valen's eyes twitched with the thought. "Star, you opened up another world to me that I didn't know existed. You set me free."

"Everyone makes their own destiny, even if you are a prince."

"And I'm ready to make mine. This is not something I do because I have to, it is done because it is necessary and honorable and I respect the privilege to serve my kingdom in the greatest way." Valen sighed, looking down at the thick carpet on the floor. "I am going to marry Vespa. It will unite both kingdoms and stall any war. In fact, it may bring peace for decades to come."

Despite the logical nature of his decision, Star felt numb and hollow inside. She knew it was inevitable and, as Valen explained, would save Ravencliff and unite the kingdoms. She did not want to see her father go to war. Besides, Valen had never said anything otherwise. He'd never proclaimed his love for her or even hinted at it at all. He had nothing to retract. It had all been unspoken, intangible, and now it was gone.

Valen took both her hands in his. "Star, I'm sorry."

She pulled away. "There is nothing to be sorry about. You've made your decision and I respect it."

He took a folded letter out of his coat pocket. "I'm sorry because I have to ask this of you. There is no one else I can trust, no one who can ride fast enough to stop the war. Star, will you deliver this letter to Vespa? Will you help me set things right?"

It was only weeks ago she'd delivered his other letter, the letter meant to break the engagement. But Star cared too much for the kingdoms and for Valen. She could not refuse. She swallowed her tears, unable to refuse. "I will."

"I have a reward for your good deeds."

Images of the ruby heart pendant hanging on the chain flitted in her memory. She felt sick. "I have no need for your rewards." Star secured the letter underneath her messenger's cloak, the white silk now stained with ash and soot. "Farewell, Your Highness." She noticed that this time he did not try to correct her formality.

With a quick bow, Star left, closing the wooden door behind her, an attendant shuffling past for more orders. She clutched her stomach as it threatened to heave. Somehow, she felt like she had lost a dear friend. But the sadness was nothing compared to the emptiness she felt in Leer's absence. With him, she'd lost more than a friend—she'd lost a love.

"What's the matter, madam?"

Star looked up to see Bellanina, hugging her bunnyfly. "Nothing." She wiped under her eyes. "Nothing, dear."

"I remember you. You saved my Flopsy." She lifted the poor animal by its armpits to show her.

Star smiled. "Yes, I did."

"Is it true what Valen says about you?"

"What does he say about me?"

"That you are a hero and you will save us from the army."

Star put her hand on the small princess's shoulder. "Don't you worry about the army."

The princess looked down, hugging the bunnyfly to her chest. She rocked her body to lull it to sleep. "But will you save us or not?"

Star's resolve came back again, an old friend she'd forgotten about resurfacing at the strangest time. "I will." She pet Flopsy between the ears and, with a wink, she set off on another quest to save the world.

Chapter 26

Message for the Queen

Star rode out before nightfall. Her return to Ravencliff lasted a mere four hours. Even Windracer issued a questioning snort when Star threw her saddle back on. But extra time could mean extra lives spent, for Evenspark's army could already be on the march. After Leer's disappearance, she did not want even one more death on her head. Not only would she deliver Valen's letter to Vespa, but she had a message for the queen, warning her about the brown-robed spies, for they'd infiltrated Evenspark, possibly hiring Zetta to carry out their ill will.

Besides, after her conversation with Valen, there was nothing for her in Ravencliff and she felt eager to leave it all behind. What was left of her family, friends and career lay in Evenspark—if she could convince the queen of the Elyndra conspiracy, the benevolence of the new King of Ravencliff, and that a bond between the kingdoms would be better than a war based on revenge.

Her list was long, and she pondered it as she rode the all-too-familiar trail leading her back to her true home. The countryside seemed vast and spacious without the blanket of mist to oppress it. Star dreamed of villages along the way—rest stops, taverns and fields where the people could farm, the merchants could trade and the poor children could grow up in a home and not a makeshift tarp. There was room for so many more people. The possibilities seemed endless and she reveled in the infinite future.

Soon the wire cage topping Evenspark Mountain came into view and Star was faced with mixed feelings about her home. The great squealing metal gates were opened but heavily guarded. Star saw scouts along the hillside, riding up and down the mossy incline with crossbows tied to their backs. Evenspark was still wary, but testing the boundaries holding it back. They were behind Ravencliff in that regard and Star whispered a silent prayer for it. At least the army hadn't marched out and she'd have a chance to change their fate.

The guards recognized her immediately, allowing her entry with wide eyes as if seeing her rise from her grave. She nodded to each one in turn, pretending she carried out a mission to deliver correspondence and nothing more.

Star looked around with apprehension. The mood in Evenspark had turned from fretful anticipation to a calm silence hanging in the air. Then she realized the mist blowers stood quiet and unused, like forgotten statues of a lost civilization, guarding the grid in mute defense. She wondered if the people of Evenspark would eventually take them down, allowing the denizens to see the vast countryside stretching beneath Evenspark's foothills, but one thought at a time. For now, she needed to get by the processing tables.

She threw her carrier's bag atop the first guarded unit. The overstuffed leather landed with a thud, raising eyes at the amount of correspondence she carried. And that was exactly what she wanted it to do. She'd brought it along with the documents from Ravencliff as a decoy to smuggle Valen's letter and her own information to the queen. After all the time she was away, she couldn't possibly turn up empty-handed.

Star did not want to face Zetta. She feared her emotions would give her intentions away. But the shrewd businesswoman surveyed the tables as always. She saw Zetta's eyes pop out and watched, slightly amused, as her superior ran out to greet her.

"My goodness! For heaven's sake, Star, you're alive!"

Star dismounted and bowed to hide the various feelings flitting through her. When she regained a stoic composure, she straightened. "I apologize for my late arrival."

"Late arrival? You're weeks behind. We thought you were dead!"

"There've been some problems with the mist as of late, but, as you can see, the trail is now clear."

Zetta looked frazzled as ever. "We don't know what went on out there, or if it's coming back. We've tried sending a few people out, but not far."

Star did not want Zetta to know the mist's disappearance was permanent, not until she'd forestalled the queen's army. For all she knew, her superior could be one of the robed people herself, but she doubted it. Zetta would not be interested in their plight. In any case, it was better to act as stupefied as they were.

"You can never be too careful. Now, I've delivered my letters to the processing tables, and I ask my leave to visit my family before they worry themselves sick."

"Of course!" Zetta eyed the letters apprehensively. Star knew she searched for the return reply from her assassination request. Unfortunately, there was no letter there for her. A sudden thought of Leer flashed in her mind and Star had to push it away. If she showed any outward emotions, she would endanger her mission, and she wanted to expose these conspirators. She owed Leer no less.

Zetta hadn't seen her wave of grief, as she was too preoccupied with the bundle of letters. "You go on, take a break if you need it. You can report back when you are ready to deliver again."

Star resisted the urge to quit then and there. With the mist gone, they could send anyone, even if they traveled on foot. She wasn't needed. Because the beasts were dead, any layman who could walk could deliver letters, but for the time being, Star had to play along. "I fear my return will be some time yet."

Zetta nodded. "Very well." She signaled a ceremonial wave good-bye. With a nod, Star jumped back onto Windracer and rode off, leaving Zetta in the dust. As she rode away, she wondered if the woman would be in a dungeon cell by the end of the day.

* * * *

Valen's letter facilitated entry into the palace. The guards recognized the royal seal of Ravencliff and allowed her to pass without question. As Star walked through the courtyard, she saw men suiting their horses, dressed in full battle armor. Flags and banners embroidered in blue with Evenspark's insignia waved in the breeze.

Star had always enjoyed watching the flags on ceremonial days, but today all the blue thread signified was bloodshed. Valen was right. The Queen of Evenspark wasted no time to exact her revenge. If she couldn't have Ravencliff by marriage, then she'd have it by force.

She quickened her pace and detoured to the queen's main audience chamber. She'd deliver Vespa's letter after dealing with the impending army. Five guards, all clad in armor with long battle swords, met her at the doorway.

Star's voice was regal and commanding as she walked straight up to the guards. "I must speak with the queen."

The guards looked to one another, uncertain. Since Tia Rood died, she was technically the head rider of Interkingdom Carriers once again, seeing she was the only adept carrier alive. Her authority outranked them all.

The oldest and tallest of the soldiers spoke. "We are on the eve of battle. The queen doesn't wish to see anyone."

Star dug out the letter with Ravencliff's seal and held it up, careful to hide the addressee. "I have official business from the King of Ravencliff."

The surprise was apparent on the soldiers' faces. One of the younger of the men's mouth actually dropped open.

"Now, if you'll let me by…"

To her relief, no one stopped her. She pushed the large oak doors open, letting fresh air breathe into the stifled room, and marched right up to the throne. The queen rose from her chair, veils wafting on the breeze and blue velvet cascading down the steps in front of her. A trio of noblewomen flanked her, all wearing headdresses like proud peacocks, gems dangling beside their faces like chimes. An old jester sat on the floor at their feet, plucking notes on a lute. Star's footsteps silenced the chatter and the melancholy tune all at once until she was the only person moving in the great hall.

The queen's voice was sharp, blowing out the veils inches from her face. "What is the meaning of this?"

"Your Highness." Star bowed when she reached earshot of the throne. "I am the head rider of the Interkingdom Carriers and I have a message from the King of Ravencliff."

"Ha!" The queen laughed. The sound was more wicked than happy. "You lie. That old man hasn't spoken one word to me in ten years."

Star straightened. "That old man you speak of is dead. I have correspondence from his son, Valen Crawford, the new King of Ravencliff."

Although the queen stood as unmoving as a faceless presence, intimidating Star more than she would have thought possible, an interest flickered in the eyes of those around them. The queen waved her long-fingered hand and everyone, jester and all, cleared out of the room.

Star waited until the last of their steps faded away before she spoke. "I have a letter from King Valen of Ravencliff stating his intentions to marry Princess Vespa. He wants to unite the two thrones once again."

"Impossible. Just two months ago he spat in our face and said the engagement was off."

Star took a deep breath, trying to keep her voice calm and informative. "Ravencliff has endured great challenges these past few days. They were attacked by the Elyndra, their walls breached. I know Valen cares for

Vespa's wellbeing, and he did not want to see her harmed. He knew it was not time for such celebrations. Their situation was perilous. He had to do what was necessary in order to keep her from danger." She produced the letter. "But it is safe now."

The queen looked her up and down, head moving underneath the veil until Star felt like the Evenspark's ruler stripped her bare, but she held fast to her words and her stance remained steady.

"How would you know what is in the letter?"

"I am but the messenger. I deliver the words of His Highness and his trusted advisors. They wanted me to know how important this delivery would be, that I could not tarry or fail, and so they told me what words I carry. In just a few days, it will be no secret. Vespa will ride to Ravencliff and our two kingdoms will be united."

Star could not persuade her so easily. "Give me the letter."

She walked up the steps to the throne and kneeled before her queen, holding the flimsy folded parchment out before her. It was one paper that could save thousands of lives. "See for yourself."

The queen ran her long fingers over the seal and scrutinized the handwriting. Star could hear her breathing change from quick intakes to long, thoughtful pauses.

"If this is true, then my army may rest again and you will be rewarded. If it is false, then you will go straight to the dungeon and be tried for treason." The queen shouted, her voice resonating through the hall. "Bring me Princess Vespa."

Chapter 27

Conspirators

Long moments passed before Princess Vespa entered the hall. Star consoled herself by calculating each minute that sped away, assuming it would prolong the release of Evenspark's army, providing Ravencliff with valuable time. But another few minutes wouldn't help anyone. It would take years for Valen to rebuild their army and the fortress wall. Evenspark's army had to be stopped altogether, and the only person that could decide was a spoiled princess. Star could only hope Vespa would accept his offer.

The main doors opened, pouring in sunlight with dust motes dancing around as a ceremonial trumpet blared. An attendant announced, "The glorious Princess Vespa of Evenspark."

The queen waved her arm, forgoing formalities. "Yes, yes. Bring her forward."

Princess Vespa waltzed in wearing a crimson gown of silk hugging all of the curves in her body before trailing to ribbons and lace on the marble floor. Her emerald eyes were alert as ever, eyebrows painted in gleaming gold glitter. In her retinue were ladies in waiting, servant girls and waiters with trays. Star wondered what they were all for.

"Your Highness." The princess bowed ever so slightly, acknowledging the one person who held authority over her. A practiced smile stretched on her luscious lips.

"Princess Vespa." The queen nodded. "This messenger brings a letter addressed to you from Valen, the new King of Ravencliff. She claims he wants your hand in marriage."

Vespa's eyes glittered with intrigue, but Star could also see a shadow of disbelief. "Did he change his mind then?"

"As it seems. This messenger claims he thought it unsafe to proceed with the marriage ceremony until they achieved victory in their battle with the Elyndra."

"I see," Vespa said. "How sweet of him." Star could not tell if she was sarcastic or serious. The princess's voice always held a haughty chime.

The queen handed the princess the letter. "You must open it now and give your answer, for my army is preparing to march."

Vespa took the letter in her hands. She ripped the seal with long, painted fingernails and read, her gaze eating the words hungrily. All stood in silence until she finished the last hasty scribbles. "It is true. He wishes for me to come to Ravencliff immediately. He assures us the mist is gone and travel is safe. We are to be married as soon as I arrive. In fact, he's preparing the ceremony festivities now as we speak."

"You will accept his offer then?" the queen asked, suddenly impatient. Some of the servant girls behind Vespa giggled.

"I will have to think on it, of course. He did have me in a fit for quite a while."

Star held her breath and the queen leaned forward, her bloodlust apparent. Star knew it would suit her just as well if Vespa refused. The fate of so many lives hung on the whim of a capricious young woman. Star hoped she'd choose love over vengeance.

However, power overrode all in the end. Vespa shrugged. "An entire kingdom. How can I refuse?" She turned to Star. "Messenger, come with me. I will write a response letter and you are to deliver it."

"I apologize, Your Highness, but you will have to find someone else. I've turned in my messenger bag for now." The last thing she wanted to do was ride back to Ravencliff and deliver Vespa's letter of love. Their marriage proceedings would have to wait until another messenger was assigned.

Vespa's tiny mouth crinkled, red lips pursing. "You can't refuse the Princess of Evenspark!"

"I'm afraid I must. I've just returned from Ravencliff to deliver this letter and policy dictates that my horse and I are entitled to a good night's rest before I can do any more riding." Star had no care as to the future of her job. They could fire her right there and it wouldn't make a difference. With the mist gone, they didn't need her anyway. No one did.

"We will find another to deliver the letter. For now, write your response." The queen gestured to the attendant at the door. "Inform the commander to put the army at ease. There will be no marching today."

"Yes, Your Highness." The attendant bowed and retreated.

Star breathed again, relief flooding her senses. She'd accomplished two out of the three objectives. The last was to inform the queen of the spies. "Your Highness, there is one more issue to address."

The queen sounded annoyed. "If you didn't just deliver the letter making my niece ruler of Ravencliff, I would send you away this very moment. But considering your past history, your status as head of Interkingdom Carriers and your connection to the throne of Ravencliff, I feel inclined to speak with you."

"My thanks, Your Highness." Star bowed again to soften her next words. "It is vital information and must be in private."

The queen once again waved everyone away. "This better be worth it." Vespa left with all of her handmaidens following like ducklings.

Once the hall cleared, Star spoke. "There are conspirators in this kingdom, people from the north who want war." She paused, gauging the queen's reaction.

"Go on."

Star had her undivided attention, and so she told her of Zetta's letter, Tia Rood's position change, the assassination attempt and, lastly, her trials at what seemed like the end of the world. She spoke of the brown-robed people, the mist machine and the end of the Elyndra.

The queen asked questions only when she needed clarification. Star left out the part about Ravencliff being defenseless. She did not want to give the queen any more inclination to attack.

"And so here I am, standing before you, asking you to question Zetta's motives and her connections." She'd given enough evidence to lock Zetta up for eternity, never mind calling her in for questioning. Now all she could do was wait for her answer.

The queen remained silent, as if she were taking it all in. "It seems these people have been meddling in our affairs for quite some time now. Do they want us all dead?"

"No. They want to control our population. They don't want our numbers to take over the planet."

"Impossible." The queen dug her nails into the wood of the throne. "How could we?"

"I asked that very same question. But the man talked of other worlds that were destroyed. He said our civilization has a propensity to multiply until there is no land or food left, that we travel from world to world, taking over until we are the only species left alive."

The queen clicked her tongue. "That is rubbish. You are certain you destroyed their mist machine?"

Star nodded. "Yes, Your Highness."

"Good." The queen sat back on her throne, one hand tracing circles in the wood of the arm rest. "Now the only thing left to do is weed them out, starting with Zetta."

"I don't think she's one of them. I think she's accepted gold in exchange for doing their dirty work. She may not be privy to the damage they have done. She is only a puppet of a larger deceit."

The queen nodded. "Perhaps. I've known Zetta's family for as long as I've lived, and not one of them has ever acted against the throne."

"We need to find her benefactor, the one behind the letters."

The queen held up a finger. "I'll have her arrested immediately. I appoint you as her chief interrogator."

Star did not know what to say. "Your Highness—"

The queen was unyielding. "You know more of this than any of us."

Star couldn't bear the cruelty of it. It would be like slamming her betrayal in her superior's face. "Your Highness, with all due respect, I do not wish to become any more entangled than I already am." She thought her refusal would bring any number of rebuttals from actually being hit to stinging words or the stripping of her title.

Instead, the queen sighed, releasing a long breath of air, and took off her veil.

Star stared as if she'd never seen with her eyes before. Underneath all the expensive fabric, the title and the nasty voice was a face of human suffering, a vulnerable monstrosity. The skin of her face stretched taut over ugly protrusions, as if pearls of all sizes were lodged underneath the outer membrane of her skin. A great, goose-egg-sized boil stuck out from above her left eyebrow, growing a few white hairs. Star couldn't bear to think of the pain and embarrassment the queen endured.

"Please," the queen said. "I cannot do it myself. What Zetta needs is to talk to a person, not a satin mask."

"All right. I'll do my best."

Chapter 28

Truth

Flickering torches lit the way down the lime-crusted steps as Star descended to question the prisoner. The dungeons of Evenspark had the same damp dreariness and insidious shadows as those in Ravencliff. Although she'd never been to Evenspark's dungeons, Star felt a wave of reminiscence and thought back to when she'd asked Leer to accompany her on her mission.

Mixed feelings of remorse, sympathy, and an unexplainable burgeoning affection blurred together. If she hadn't asked him, then he wouldn't be dead. Yet she would have never succeeded in her quest without him and they would have never had that time together. She would have never felt his lips on her own as his passion for her spilled out in the last moments of his burdened life.

Star sighed. She was so heartsick she was in no mood to question anyone, let alone her superior, yet Zetta waited for her in a cell in the deepest bowels of the dungeons. She had to carry on with her mission, whether she wanted to or not. Besides, it just might give her a reprieve from the immense feelings blossoming then withering in her heart.

The guard nodded when she approached and opened the heavy wooden door with a heave. "She's all yours. Won't talk to anyone, so good luck."

Star stepped into the cell and saw Zetta sitting in the corner on a pile of old hay. She had her legs folded up against her chest and her arms wrapped around them, as if she could hide from the world. Star felt a pang of pity, for Zetta was there because of her. She'd turned her in red-handed.

Zetta looked up at her with wary eyes. Her gaze turned to recognition and loathing. "Star! Are you behind all of this? Did you report my private letter?"

"I am and I did."

Aubrie Dionne

"But why? Why get involved? Why not do as you're told and let life go on as normal?"

Anger flared in Star's chest. "Because those letters carried the downfall of both kingdoms."

"That's impossible. They were going to the outskirts. No one there has power or authority over anyone."

Star realized Zetta had no idea who she enabled. She'd thought it was a favor for a nobleman, an inconsequential private task. Star had to remind herself Zetta still cheated the system.

"Zetta, listen to me, this is very important. Who asked you to deliver those letters?"

Her superior shrugged. "I didn't catch a name."

This would be harder than she thought. Star sat across from Zetta. She was already so journey-worn and dirty the dungeon floor couldn't possibly make her appearance any worse. "Zetta, the people behind the letters are conspirators against both Evenspark and Ravencliff."

"Nonsense. The letters were addressed to Fallon Leer. I've met the man myself. He was one of our best riders, before you came along, and has a heart kinder than any man I've ever known. He'd never do anything against his kingdom."

With the mention of Leer's name, Star reeled. Tears stung her eyes and she blinked them back. Now was not the time to show vulnerability. "Zetta, Fallon is dead. He died helping me fight the Elyndra. He intercepted these letters in an attempt to find the people involved."

Zetta's voice caught. "Leer is dead?"

Star couldn't talk about Leer, not now. She had avoided uttering his name for fear the dam holding back her emotions would burst, but Zetta forced her to come to terms with her imminent feelings and his martyred death. "Yes, and if you don't tell me who's behind the letters, then he died fighting a lost cause. His mission will never be complete."

Zetta stared her down, penetrating her eyes, searching for deception. She muttered, "My God, you loved him."

Star wiped back her tears, ignoring Zetta's claim. "Please, Zetta, tell me who sent those letters."

Zetta sat back, releasing her legs. She waited a moment before taking a deep breath, as if she launched herself into a journey of her own. "The first time I saw the brown-robed man, he lurked in the shadows of the night. He scared me. I thought he was a robber, but instead of holding out a knife, he held a bag of gold. He said it was imperative his letters were sent privately, that they not be processed by the system. He had no identification tags, and so would not be allowed to send them."

Zetta rubbed her face, accidentally smudging dirt on her forehead. Star could tell she'd struggled with the decision to accept his bargain.

"Did you ask why he had no tags?"

"No." Zetta sighed. "With that much gold, you don't ask questions. My family has scraped the bottom of our savings for years ever since a rich uncle diverted our inheritance to hoard it for himself. I needed the money."

"Did you get any notion of where he was from? Where he was staying? Anything?"

"All I know is he smelled strange, like potions and chemicals. He had a snobbish quality to his speech and persona, like he thought himself far superior than us lowly Interkingdom Carriers. But I accepted his money nonetheless."

Star chewed on her lower lip. He sounded much like the man she met in the machine before the orb absorbed his body. Everything in Zetta's story checked out. Star would write a report for the queen dismissing Zetta's involvement as minimal and naming the perpetrators as the robed people from the north. "Zetta, this is especially important. When did you see him last?"

Zetta blew out air from her mouth. "Weeks ago. Right before I sent you out with that letter addressed to Leer."

Star pursed her lips. That meant the spy could be anywhere by now. In fact, he could have perished with all the rest of them back at the machine. Now all they could do was pick up the pieces and be alert in case any of them still lived and tried something in the future.

She gave Zetta a sad smile. "I will do my best to annul your crimes. I can't guarantee you will be set free, but I will speak on your behalf."

Zetta came forward, taking Star's hand in both of hers. "I thank you so very much. All I've caused you is pain. We both knew that Tia Rood was unfit to be a messenger. I chose her because she didn't question my orders. I replaced you, yet you still fight for my rights?"

Star felt her heart warm. She'd forgiven the spry old woman. "We must unite against these conspirators. You are not the enemy. Besides, I don't think they'll be back anytime soon." She rose up from the hay, dusting off her messenger's cloak and knocked on the door of the cell to be let out.

"The robed people, what did they want?"

Star turned back to face her, her face drawn and her eyes heavy. "They wanted most of us dead."

Zetta furrowed her eyebrows. "That just doesn't make sense at all."

"Wait until you hear the rest of it."

The guard opened the cell door, and nothing more could be said. With a swift nod, Star walked away, leaving Zetta to do what she did best—worry and brood.

She filed the report that evening, requesting Zetta be released under oath to abide by the rules of the Interkingdom Carriers. She'd be watched from afar to see if the brown-robed man returned, but Star knew he was long gone by now. She also suspected Zetta would be wary to accept any other offers.

Star could hardly believe she'd reached the end of her arduous journey. She had nowhere left to go but home. Walking Windracer behind her, Star followed the all-too-familiar streets to her family's home in the outskirts. As she passed by the metal structure of the grid, she could see through the weave work to the land beyond.

Although the Forgotten One's story was ridiculous, Star felt there must be some kernel of truth. Why else would he stand by his convictions, right up until his imminent death? She didn't like to think about it because there was only one choice she could have made. Perhaps she had doomed them all to extinction in thousands of years, but at least now she knew her parents and the people of Ravencliff and Evenspark were safe.

Chapter 29

Unexpected Visitor

"Whatever happened with the man that gave you the ruby necklace?" Star's mother asked as she brought out a bowl of hot stew.

Star huddled under a homespun quilt in her father's old armchair in her bedroom and shrugged, trying to look nonchalant. "It didn't work out."

"I see." Her mother set down the steaming bowl. "There are many other suitors out there, and you are such a beautiful young woman."

Star resisted the urge to frown. She didn't want other suitors and she didn't want Valen. The man she sought lay beyond her reach now.

Her mother squeezed her shoulder with tearful eyes. "It's good to have you back home. Have some stew. You'll feel much better."

Star summoned as much of a smile as possible before her mother disappeared into the kitchen. She didn't think anything would get much better, even after eating the stew. She'd lost everything, including her job, her first love interest and the man she realized she truly loved in the end. She didn't even have the ruby necklace to sell. Her family was as poor as they ever were, and she'd given up on moving them to the inner district, though with the mist gone, it didn't matter. The Interkingdom Carriers weren't knocking on her door, and her good deeds were all but forgotten with the talk of the wedding uniting both kingdoms. Ravencliff considered Star a hero, but that was the last place she ever wanted to go back to again.

She resigned herself to the inner rooms of her parents' house for the next week, where she folded clothes, peeled potatoes, and tried to mend the ache in her body and her heart. She felt empty inside, like her insides were tossed around and mixed up, and now her thoughts were all mush. She'd been consumed by her quest to the point where everyone and everything was secondary, and now that she'd finished it, she had nothing left, for she'd lost so much in order to achieve her success. Yes, she saved the world, but it was a hollow triumph with no one to share it.

* * * *

Buttons flashed and steam spouted behind her. Star's fingers touched the cool metal wall of the corridor. Her hand was a beige blur in the reflection. She could hear the hum of the machine in between beeps of a warning alarm.

Star looked around her, time pressing on her shoulders. Maybe if she got out fast enough she would be able to save Leer. She flung herself down the corridor. Her arms tangled in strange, snakelike coils sparking and whizzing, and her legs stumbled over bodies. So many robed people lay dead at her feet. But her one concern was for Leer.

When she reached the entranceway, the flames raged beneath her. She saw his black cloak disappear into them and lunged forward with all of her might, flying through the haze of smoke. Her hands groped, but her fingers only brushed the fabric and soon it disappeared, eaten by the orange tongues that licked the air.

"No!" she screamed as the cloak melted into ashes. She fanned the flames with her bare arms, trying to reach through to drag him out, but her skin caught fire and she fell back, beating her arm against the earth. Pain flared, the skin bubbling with ugly boils, but the devastation raging through her heart overshadowed any physical pain. She realized then Leer had opened his heart to her in the cave before he left and she'd given him nothing in return. She never got a chance to tell him how she really felt. He died thinking she loved Valen.

Star fell to her knees and covered her ears, sobbing. All at once, the hollering sound of wind and fire disappeared, leaving her in bare silence.

* * * *

Star sat up groggily and recognized the comforting walls of her family's house. The sun had set, leaving her in shadows.

"You all right, honey?" her mother called.

"Yes, I'm fine. Come in."

The door opened gently and her mother came in with a lantern and a glass of water. "Sounds like you were having a nightmare."

Star looked down at her hands expecting to see ash and blood, but there was nothing there. "I was."

"You always did have nightmares as a child." Her mother patted her head, smoothing over the tangles in her hair. "That's why you were so driven to ride out. You wanted to face your fears head on."

Star smiled. "I was such a stubborn girl."

"And you still are." Her mother kissed her head. "And I love you all the more for it."

A sudden knock came at the front door.

"I'll get it." Her father's voice came from the study.

Her mother furrowed her eyebrows, a bit annoyed. "Who could that be at this time of night?"

Star had a moment of hope that the Interkingdom Carriers needed her back, but that was soon overshadowed by the fact she didn't want to return to Ravencliff. Besides, she'd heard in town that the Interkingdom Carriers had stripped Zetta of her title and people made their own deliveries. There were more and more riders vying for jobs. Star was now one in a hundred. The chance someone needed a delivery sent was as slim as the chance that an Elyndra would ever fly again in the sky.

Her father entered her bedroom with a quizzical look on his sun-browned face. "There's a man at the door to see you." He rubbed his temple. Star knew he'd been reading too long as always. However, the gesture was not just tired eyes. A hint of worry showed in the wrinkle between his white brows.

Her mother put a hand to her heart. "Oh, maybe it's the man who gave you the necklace? Maybe he's changed his mind?"

Star shook her head, resisting the urge to scold her mother. "No, Mother. He's decided to marry someone else."

"Then who else could it be?"

Her father's eyes held suspicion. "He looked rather shady, tattoos on his arm and black clothes like a delinquent."

Star stood from the chair in disbelief, the quilt falling to the floor at her feet. Weeks had passed since her journey and it couldn't possibly be true. "Did he say his name?"

Her father shrugged. "Said you'd know him when you saw him. I don't know, Star, he seems a bit devious to me. Do you want me to send him away?"

Star didn't answer her father's question. She leaped forward, her feet tangled in the quilt and kicked the fabric off impatiently, sprinting down the hallway to the door. Her head told her it couldn't be true, but her heart wished it so a thousand times over.

She opened the door and gaped as Fallon Leer stood on the porch, leaning casually on the railing like he lived there himself.

"Seems you've been telling people I'm dead." A smug grin crossed his face as he straightened to meet her. He favored his right leg, as if his left were made of stone. A cane rested at his side.

Aubrie Dionne

Star could not speak. She closed the distance between them and fell into his arms, holding him close, as if he were a dream that would fly away on the wind, but he felt so real, his broad arms and back solid underneath her embrace. Her tears fell onto his chest as she buried her face into his warmth. For a second, he stood motionless, as if he didn't know what to do, and then his arms came around her, comforting her sobs. He soothed her by rubbing a hand up and down her back.

When she regained a slim amount of composure, Star studied his face. He had a slight scar on his cheek and a burn mark on his neck. Besides that, he was all in one piece. She brought her hand up to his scar and traced it gently with her fingertips. "It can't be."

"The funny thing is, one of those Elyndra picked me up into the sky just as the flames started to close in around me. I let it carry me out of that vile hole in the earth to the rim. Once I was free, I stabbed it in the stomach and the beast dropped me several feet to the ground."

"But I looked for you for days, calling out your name."

As always, Leer's response was simple and to the point. "Unconscious."

"My goodness, for how long?"

"Don't know, but when I woke up, I was thirsty as all hell and sore."

Star feared his answer to her next question, but she had to ask. "And Wildfire?"

Leer looked off into the distance, his eyes flitting back and forth. "Gone."

"Oh, Leer, I'm so sorry."

"It's all right. He completed his task and died valiantly. I always knew he was destined for a greater purpose. I was just borrowing him until his time came."

"How did you make it back without Wildfire?"

Leer smiled sadly. "I had to trudge all the way back with a broken leg. It took days. By the time I got to Ravencliff, you were already gone."

Star felt guilt redden her face. "I'm sorry I left you. I thought you were dead."

"I should have been. Lucky, that's what I was. I figured you were on your way. I followed your trail of campfires all the way back to Ravencliff."

"I told Valen you were to go down as a hero."

"And he gave me more credit than I deserve. When I got back, they were already planning a statue in my honor." He laughed lightly. "Don't know if I'll still get it now I'm alive."

"You should. You should get more."

Leer smiled. "I don't much care about all that. I achieved what I wanted to. That is, I paid my debt back to Valen and saved his kingdom. He can no longer look down upon me." He sighed. "I can never change what I did, never bring back his mother, but in my own way, I've done enough to set it right."

Star knew it wouldn't be worth it to argue with him. Even though it had never been entirely his fault and Valen had forgiven him long ago, she knew it was something he had to do to clear his own conscience. She allowed him that entitlement without judgment or complaint.

Leer looked down into the folds of her blouse. "So, you still wear that ridiculous ruby necklace?"

Star pulled back, insulted, and loosened her grip. "Of course not! I used it to destroy the machine. Anyway, didn't you hear that Valen is marrying Princess Vespa?"

"I did. But I had to see what you thought of it."

She didn't want him to think she still cared for Valen like that. She unbuttoned the top snaps of her blouse. "Look for yourself what lies next to my heart."

Leer paused as if she was about to trick him. He narrowed his eyes and shook his head, as if it was beyond the bounds of propriety.

"Go on."

His rough, calloused hand gently pulled back the cotton fabric, fingers tickling her skin. He found the chain around her neck and pulled the accessory until it came into full sight. He blinked as though his eyes lied. She still wore his identification tags. Leer looked at her in a different way, as if he saw her for who she truly was for the first time. "But these are mine. I left them in the cave."

"When you were gone, I realized how much I'd grown to care for you. Fallon, I love you."

Leer put his hand up to hold her face, admiring her like she was too good to be true. Star raised her hand and placed her fingertips on his lips. She brushed his mouth with her fingers before bracing her hands on either side of his head. Reaching up, she touched her lips to his.

He kissed her back, softly at first, then with more passion as they settled into their embrace. Star responded to each movement, melting into his arms. Her hands roamed through his hair, brushing his neck and smoothing over his shoulders.

She heard movement inside the house and remembered where she stood, on her parents' porch. She pulled back, feeling a bit embarrassed.

Aubrie Dionne

Leer, on the other hand, was not shy at all. "On my way to Evenspark, I claimed several acres of land in the highlands, above the swamp where the earth is good for grazing. I want to start a horse ranch, build a house in the country." He pointed to the tattoos on his arm. "It's been my dream all my life to train a herd of wild horses, to ride across the countryside."

Star ran a finger up his arm, curving around the head of an Appaloosa. "And?"

"I'm asking you to come with me. You wouldn't be far from here, just a few hours' ride. But it would be outside of the grid."

Star couldn't believe it. What he proposed sounded like a paradise.

"I need someone who's good with horses and—"

She spoke, almost breathless. "The answer is yes."

Star never saw Leer smile the way he did right then. It was as if she'd righted all the wrongs in his life with one word.

"Come in and meet my parents. My mom will make you dinner." Star winked playfully, tugging his arm toward the front door. "She's an excellent cook."

Leer rolled his eyes, allowing himself to be pulled. "I'm sure they'll adore me."

Star turned back around, her lips curved upward in a tease. "You rode to the end of the mist, set fire to the cocoons and stabbed an Elyndra as it took you away. And now you're afraid of my parents."

Leer looked ashamed, like a boy caught playing with his father's tools. "Not afraid. I just don't think they'll like me, that's all. I'm not the typical knight in shining armor you'd be proud to bring home."

"No, you're not." His reluctance made him even more irresistible to Star. She smoothed a hand over his chest. "You're much better."

Chapter 30

Double Weddings

Rose petals rained down in the throne room, falling between the banners of both kingdoms. For once in a century of uneasy politics, the insignias were intertwined, embroidered together by the deftest weavers in all the land. Spectators from both factions filled the great hall, every inch taken by a distant cousin, a wandering merchant or a soldier in the royal guard. Doves fluttered overhead, set free by jesters as they twirled and spiraled, delighting the crowd.

A noblewoman turned to her friend. "I heard they'd been secretly engaged since birth."

Her friend raised her slender eyebrows. "Is that so? I heard he cut it off to safeguard her life because he knew of the Elyndras' impending attack."

"How valiant of him."

The second woman polished her pearl necklace. "Valiance is Valen's greatest attribute. Some people even say that it's his middle name."

"Hmm. And what do we know of Vespa?"

"She is beautiful beyond measure, possessing fine-boned traits given to her by her father, nobleman of Ravencliff, and sturdy as a man in spirit, an attribute all rulers in the house of Evenspark possess."

"I see. That makes for quite the pairing indeed."

"I only hope Valen stands his ground."

Valen waited before the throne, golden crown glinting as the sun shone on him through painted-glass windows. He wore a ceremonial baldric with the scarlet and ebony colors of Ravencliff and a velvet cape that fell to the very bottom of the raised platform. A graveness painted his face.

He looked back to his best man, Allyn, the new commander-in-chief of Ravencliff's army. Although young, he'd served bravely in the war and Valen made sure he would follow in his family's tradition. Both of them had lost a father in the battle, but Valen would see to it that it had all been for a higher purpose. They would not have died in vain.

Allyn nodded formally, expressing his support of the alliance between kingdoms. It seemed the entire board of advisors, the army, the citizens and the other nobles of the castle agreed with his decisions as the new ruler. If anything, Valen won their respect—more than what his father had achieved. As many differences as they had, Valen still wished his father were there on such a momentous day. Looking up above, he knew his father's spirit shined down on the ceremony and that he soared with pride.

A band of minstrels strummed a regal march, trumpets resounding to the upper rafters where the long-forgotten webs of spiders wafted on the breeze. The doors opened and Bellanina came out first, dropping roses at the onlookers' feet. She paced solemnly, head up to the altar, as if she were already practicing for her own coronation.

Vespa entered next, wearing a satin gown of snow white with rubies stitched into the hem. Handmaidens had twined her auburn hair in one hundred braids, every delicate strand strategically placed in interlocking circles forming an intricate bun.

She gazed at Valen and the throne that lay beyond him and her eyes glittered, refracting the sun like multifaceted emeralds. She marched forward to claim the title of queen, handmaidens holding her dress so it spread behind her like wings. Each step brought her closer to her title. When she met Valen, she bowed once, ever so slightly, to acknowledge him, before her hungry eyes gleamed at the crown shining on an ivory pedestal by the priest.

The music came to a lull, trumpets giving way to the silence of the impending ceremony. The priest lit the two smaller tapered candles beside the unity candle in the middle of the hall.

Valen bent down and whispered in Vespa's ear, "I'm glad you accepted my offer."

Vespa looked back with a challenge. "I could not refuse."

* * * *

On the same day, a kingdom away, Leer stood on a hillside, overlooking the green land of his new horse ranch. A small group of bystanders surrounded him, including Star's parents, some Interkingdom Carriers, and a few aunts and uncles.

An elderly man plucked delicate chords on a lute, accompanied by the sweet whistle of a recorder. Sparrows flew overheard in the dome of a blue sky, void of clouds. The crowd looked to the bottom of the incline, beyond the wild lavender and daises to a single woman, hair white as snow and eyes gray as a storm cloud. She wore a simple dress of blue that matched the cloudless sky, her translucent hair trailing behind her on the light wind.

Star blushed as she paced up the path of the hill, holding a bouquet of foxglove and evening primrose. This scene was not what she'd envisioned several months ago before she had met Leer. In fact, it was quite the opposite, but in all ways it was better. Here she was, out in the open plains, with no fear and no worries from above. The man standing on the top of the hill shared her love for horses. He was everything she trained to be, an excellent rider with a bold sense of honor and a kind heart. In many ways, they were two halves of the same fruit, growing up in the outskirts to rise above their setbacks and make a difference in the world. Besides the obvious things in common, there was so much love it threatened to overwhelm both of them every day. Her heart swelled as her emotions ran unbidden. Star would remember this day for the rest of her life.

Behind her, Windracer snorted, bringing her thoughts back to the present. The crowd laughed and the solemn mood lightened.

"Shush, Windracer," she whispered under her breath. "You'll still be my age-old friend."

She rounded the bend in the path and her gaze met Leer's. He smiled his own crooked, half-twitching of the lips that could only mean he'd won in the end. She grinned warmly when she reached his side. Maybe he did win, but she won as well.

"I've loved you since the first day I saw you," Leer whispered with intensity burning in his eyes. "I never thought I'd be worthy of such a woman, such a wife."

"And I'd never thought I'd find another so like myself. I've loved you since you showed your true self, the shape of your heart," Star responded as the minister lit the candles and the audience hushed, awaiting the ceremony.

"I don't show that to too many people. I can't risk my reputation now."

Star took his arm, teasing. "It's way too late for that."

Meet the Author

Aubrie Dionne writes fantasy and science fiction for young adults and adults. As a girl, she collected horse statues and looked forward to getting mail. Messenger in the Mist comes from her admiration of horses and expert riders, and her love of the written word.
Her stories can be found at Lyrical Press, Gypsy Shadow Publishing and SynergEbooks. She's also published short fiction in Niteblade, Silver Blade, Aurora Wolf and Emerald Tales. Please visit her blog to say hi: http://authoraubrie.blogspot.com.

Aubrie's Website:
www.authoraubrie.com
Reader eMail:
aubriedionne@yahoo.com